To my mum for giving me a love of
books and my dad for giving me
a love of *Star Trek*.

'*It's life, Captain, but not as we know it.*'

Commander Spock,

Star Trek: The Motion Picture

Not As We Know It

Tom Avery

Illustrated by Kate McKendrick Grove

Andersen Press · London

Treasure

A storm came to Portland. In the night it threw itself against our windows. The thunder called to us. Black clouds gathered across the island. The days were dark.

When storms are finished, Chesil Beach – the stony bank that connects our island to the mainland – is always littered. Driftwood, tangled balls of fishermen's nets, glass bottles and plastic packets, all lie like God's rubbish, spilt from a heavenly bin bag.

There's treasure, too. Ned and I go searching amongst the junk. We claim the choicest gems, make them our prize, take them home to our trove.

Dad's low garage has never been big enough

for his van. It's a wrinkled-metal building that doesn't hold a car either. Instead, it's bursting with the salvage of a dozen storms.

We have collected shoes in all sizes, from a baby's leather bootie to a yellow rubber wader. There's a box of bones that sits on a high shelf, topped with a cow's skull. In an old paint tin stands a rusted and broken knife, as long as my forearm. Three forks rattle in the tin when we fetch it down; we are always on the lookout for spoons.

Hats and a leather bag with a golden clasp. A little whale, carved from bone. Unopened cans of food, all label-less. A hairbrush. Children's toys and books swollen and cracked by the sea's waves and sun's rays. All kinds of fishermen's tackle hangs about a life-ring that probably saved no one's life.

Some things took both of us to drag back along

the shingle: a bicycle frame; a chair with a missing leg; a long, thick oar; a metal tub, like a small bath that sits in the very middle of the garage.

Once we found the rotted carcass of a seal. Ned said we should take it home as part of our '*mission to seek out new life*'. The light was failing by the time we got it off the beach and up, up the coast path to our stone cottage and brick garage. Mum made us bury it.

As ever, with this latest storm, we'd waited, watched the lightning, whooped at the crack of thunder. The storm passed and Dad left early for work. One fence panel was down. Mum said to fix it before I thought about doing anything else. I pushed it into place and nailed it to the post. I could hear Ned, inside on the sofa, coughing his lungs up as Mum beat on his chest. I hammered harder and hummed the *Star Trek* theme tune.

Anthony, one of our neighbours, Dad's mate, beeped his horn as he drove past. I waved. He winked and nodded, his policeman's helmet bobbing up and down.

From next door, Mrs Clarke called over the fence, 'Will you keep it down!'

'Sorry. I'm nearly finished.'

She huffed, closed the door and returned to her kitchen, glaring from the window.

I hammered the last nail in place as Ned, his treatment over, flew through the front door. Free, we mounted our bikes and free-wheeled them down the long hill before leaving them where the beach began.

'Come on,' my brother called, crunching along the top of the bank.

The sky is always deepest blue after nights of wind and rain. I could see only blue and blue and

Ned's scrawny body, scrabbling away from me.

My brother began the usual introduction to our hunt, borrowed from our favourite programme: *'These are the adventures of Ned and Jamie.'*

I joined in, laughing and putting on my best Captain Kirk voice. *'Their continuing mission to explore strange new places, to seek out new life and junk on the beach. To boldly go,'* I shouted.

'Where no man has gone before,' Ned finished, and we chuckled as we kept on trekking.

Our sack was empty. Our eyes scanned the shoreline. Ned's thin plimsolls kicked through the flotsam.

'Get off,' he said to a strand of brown seaweed that clung to his leg. He shook it till a coughing fit took over.

The gulls crawked above us. Maybe if I'd

listened carefully, I'd have heard them call a warning. *Beware*.

When Ned was done, I knelt and peeled the weed from his bony ankle. 'Home? We could try again later,' I said. I didn't want to go home, but some things are more important than what I want.

Ned pulled the face that said he was fine, eyebrows up, big smile drawn from ear to ear. 'We haven't got anything yet,' he said.

I eyed my brother, scratched my chin, then nodded.

We climbed back to the top of the bank. We stood a while, breathed the salty air and watched the cars, ferrying people on and off the island along the road parallel to the coast. Then our searching gazes followed the long curve of the beach to where the frothy sea met pebbles.

A fisherman, his long pole spiking up and out

towards the sea, stood within shouting distance. A couple, hand in hand, trudged towards us from the island. Apart from those few, the beach was ours.

We stared at a murky patch of browns and greens, beyond the fisherman. A tangled web of seaweed like that could hold treasure. Or it could be ten minutes wasted, picking through slime.

'Let's do it,' Ned said.

We kept to the crest of the gravel wave, taking slow steps. The beach moved beneath our feet, stones running away down each side, towards the English Channel on our left and Weymouth Harbour on our right.

'Mornin',' the fisherman called as we passed above him.

'Morning,' I said in my voice.

'*Mornin',*' Ned said in the fisherman's voice, deep and gravelly.

The fisherman turned away and shook his head as Ned giggled.

When we got to the patch, the weeds were deep. They swamped our shoes as we used our feet to search, pushing the plants aside, uncovering the beach beneath. There were the usual nets and scraps of rubbish, plastic and glass and string.

I waded deeper, squelching through the murky brown till my left foot fell on something that was neither rock nor weed.

'Maybe something here,' I called, taking a step back.

Ned coughed towards me. I prodded with a rubber toe. It was soft, fleshy. I pushed the weeds aside. Beneath was dark brown, smooth and shimmering.

'What is it?' Ned said at my elbow.

I crouched and put a finger to our find. Smooth

to the eye but some roughness to the touch, like skin. I pushed harder and felt movement beneath.

'It's alive,' I hissed at my brother. 'Maybe another seal.'

Ned lowered himself next to me and we gently plucked away the layers of seaweed. The brown skin became scaled with green and blue in one direction and a deeper brown – almost black – the other.

'Some sort of fish?' Ned whispered.

We pulled at the weeds, uncovering a rectangle of flesh, smooth at one end, scaled the other. It's the creature's back, I thought.

This gave way to limbs and joints not like a fish's. They were tiny, no longer than a baby's. They looked shrunken connected to long hands and feet – as long as Grandad's, longer than most men's. But where Grandad's hands were wide fillets, these were slim and the bones beneath stick-thin.

Ned and I were silent. The sea fell silent. Above, the seagulls no longer spoke. Maybe they stared down too. A few strands of green and brown weed remained, where a head should be, could be.

'Wait,' I hissed as my brother reached forwards. 'What is it?'

Ned grinned. 'Let's find out.'

My heart hammered. I wanted to pile the seaweed back over our find, turn and crunch away to discover old shoes and maybe that missing spoon. I wanted things to stay as they were.

But my brother wanted adventure. He always

did. He pulled back the last thin fronds.

My stomach rose up and stopped my breath. I was filled with terrible fear and thunderous excitement.

I'd never seen a head like this. The creature was on its side. Its eyes were closed but human in shape and the nose was the small button nose of a child. There the human ended and the fish began. Its mouth was wide, stretching round from one side of the face to the other. Below this and the long narrow jaw were closed gills. On the top, where hair should have been, was a row of three pronged fins. No ears.

We crouched and stared as the tiny back rose and fell and the creature breathed long, silent breaths.

With my eyes wide and my heart pounding against my chest, like one of the massive drills

Dad used at the quarry, I glanced at my brother. Ned's face was alight with excitement.

I looked back to the creature. Neither of us spoke.

We stared as an eye cracked open, an eye as black as the deepest sea, and one of those long, thin hands shot out and grabbed Ned's wrist. Our creature pulled itself towards him with the faintest croak and perhaps a flicker of recognition.

We both screamed. Ned wrenched away and we fell back into the mess of slimy weeds. The creature fell back too. And the eye closed.

Home

Our grandad is a seaman. He's lived his whole life on or near the deep blue. He's hauled cargo back and forth across the seas, on a ship longer than our street. He captained a trawler, heaving tonnes of mackerel and herring and sprat ashore. Later he dived for scallops, bringing those crusty shells up from the deep. He isn't retired. Just on an extended break.

I think Dad's job as a quarryman is a disappointment to Grandad. He always says, 'I am married to the sea. Your father's married to the rock and stone.'

Grandad brings us great slabs of fish: a choice plaice, a Dover sole, the largest pollock you've ever seen. A forty-pounder he reckoned. Grandad taught us to gut and de-bone, fillet, butterfly. Once, he tried to teach me and Ned to suck the eye from a fish's socket.

Ned had tapped his chest and said, 'Sorry, Grandad, just feeling a bit congested today.' My brother laughed.

I managed a grin; Ned's chest wasn't something to laugh about.

Grandad asked me what my excuse was. He didn't make me suck out any eyeballs, though.

So, growing up with all that fish around, all that squelchy flesh, it wasn't squeamishness that made us hesitate before bundling our find into the sack. It was fear. There was fear pulsing through both of us.

We gulped air as we pulled ourselves up from the weeds.

'I'll get . . . I'll get . . . Grandad,' I said.

Ned stared at the thing, at the being. He didn't answer for a long moment. The sea's crash rose in our ears again, a wild call.

'No,' my brother said at last. 'This is *our* find. It's our find. We'll take him home first.'

That word, *'first'*. *I* heard, *First* we'll take him home, then we'll tell someone. But *Ned* meant, *First* we'll take him home, then we'll see what we'll see.

So we bundled the tiny man into the sack. Ned rolled him gently as I held the bag open.

'Watch the mouth. It might bite,' I said.

The creature's cold, wet skin brushed against my fingers. No hair. Scales and skin and skeleton beneath.

I shuddered at the cold, at the wild.

✱

'Find anything good,' the fisherman called as we stepped lightly back along the ridge.

'Erm,' I said with an urge to shout, *We've found a living thing. Something awesome and terrible.*

Ned coughed, not his usual wet rattle. 'Just shoes and stuff,' he said.

The fisherman sniffed, nodded and returned to his rod.

I pulled and turned the sack. The creature wasn't heavy. It was terrifyingly light, like its bones were hollow. Its pointed elbow dug into my back.

The couple smiled at us as we passed. I didn't smile back. Ned did, brightly beaming.

Usually we tied the sack to my handlebars and it clattered along against my front wheel as we ground our way up the hill. I did not think our little creature would thank us for the bruises though.

'You wheel the bikes,' my brother said. 'I'll carry Leonard.'

'Leonard?'

Ned's pet crab had been called Leonard, after his favourite member of the starship *Enterprise* crew, Leonard 'Bones' McCoy. We'd kept it in the tub in the garage until the water turned green and we found Leonard still and unmoving. We'd buried the crab alongside the seal.

If Ned wanted to call the creature Leonard, we'd call it Leonard. Ned usually had his way.

I wheeled the bikes, one in each hand. Ned carried Leonard.

There's a spot, halfway up, where a second path leaves ours, going quickly down, scrabbling and hopping from rock to rock to a platform, thrusting into the sea. A spot where we always stop. On that clear day we stared back down along the beach, the sea on both sides of it. We could see far beyond Weymouth.

We'd walked the whole beach once, the eighteen long miles. Just me and Ned. On a day he'd wanted to escape. We'd had to get the bus back. Not cos Ned moaned – Ned never moaned – but I could see when he winced that his knees were bad and his coughing had got worse with every mile. I told him I was too tired for the walk back, otherwise he would have insisted he was fine and stumbled and coughed all the way home, or fallen somewhere along the lonely bank. When we got back, Dad was angrier than I'd ever seen him. Mum just cried. We haven't walked it again. Now we just gazed back along it.

The fisherman was still there. Two more had joined him, dots on the shingle.

'Come on,' I said, stooping to attack the last five hundred metres.

Ned coughed and wheezed behind me. We left the path onto our tiny road with its handful of cottages, their backs to the English Channel.

I was glad Mrs Clarke wasn't by her garden gate; she always quizzed us on what we were up to.

Mum saw us from the kitchen. I watched her turn down the radio and open the window.

'Is he all right?' she called to me.

'I'm fine,' Ned replied.

'Come in soon,' she said.

We nodded and waved.

We knew where we would put the creature. Without talking, we dumped our bikes by the front gate. Ned opened the side door of the garage. The old hinges squeaked.

'In the tub,' Ned said.

Once I'd removed it from the sack, we stared again. We stared a long time, Ned wheezing.

There's only two other kids on our road – Lucy, my friend, who was in our class when we went to school, and her little brother Peter. Peter's tiny, even for a three-year-old. Lucy calls him Peewee.

Laid out in the little tub, Leonard was no taller than Peewee. So slender. Skinnier than Ned. His colours startled again, from darkest brown to bright blue and purple.

'What is it?' I said.

'Not it. Leonard,' Ned replied.

'What is Leonard?'

We didn't know. We knew he was a sea creature. That was it. For the first time the word *merman* swam into my mind. I did not let it dive out of my mouth.

I fetched the hose that lived attached to the outside tap. Ned tried to turn it on.

'I've loosened it for you, Jamie,' he said when I took over.

We let a trickle of cold water fall on Leonard's chest. The little man shivered, not a chill shiver but one of relief. I turned the tap on fully and Ned placed the hose at the end of the tub, away from Leonard.

'He's a sea creature, right? He'll need salt,' Ned said.

I nodded. 'Mum's got sea salt. In the kitchen,' I replied.

I turned the tap back off and fetched the salt. Mum was upstairs; I had no questions to answer. Yet.

When I returned, Ned was crowded over the tub, ready to join the fish-man.

'How much?' I asked.

'Here,' Ned said, taking the salt and emptying in a handful.

I went outside and turned the tap once more.

We stood and watched the bath fill. The water covered Leonard's hands and feet first.

'They're the same,' Ned said.

His hands and feet were almost identical. Feet-like hands and hand-like feet. Both long, jointed and scaled. As they spread in the cool water, I could see the webbing that connected each one to its neighbour.

The water covered his chest and stomach where the brown skin gave way to scaled legs.

'Look,' Ned said.

The gills on Leonard's neck opened and closed and opened again.

Every time Ned had to stay off school for a week or two or more, Dad would buy a new *Star Trek* video. We've got the whole set now. All three series. All seventy-nine episodes aboard the USS *Enterprise*.

One of my favourites has these creatures called tribbles. The tribbles seem harmless. They are small, fluffy balls that purr and quiver. But they multiply and spread all over the spaceship. They get everywhere. The episode's called 'The Trouble with Tribbles'.

Our fish-man was not a tribble. Leonard, lithe and slimy, looked nothing like them. But like them, he seemed innocent. Harmless. We'd taken him in, like the *Enterprise* crew had taken on the tribbles. As we stared mesmerised, I could not help but think of all the trouble Leonard might cause.

Then we heard footsteps. Ned leaped up.

'Come on, boys. I want you in,' Mum called as the squeak of hinges sounded over the bubbling water.

'Wait,' my brother shouted, running for the door.

Story

'We're coming in,' Ned said, bundling Mum out before she had the door open, before she saw into the garage.

'Let's go, you've got work to do!' she said.

We hadn't been to school for months as Mum wanted us home. She wanted to look after Ned there. It had been early summer when we stopped going to school. The date was inked in my mind – 5 May 1983. The date marked a change, a big change for Ned, for what was happening to him.

'Maybe they'll come back after the summer holiday,' Dad had told the head teacher. 'We'll see how Ned's doing.'

We didn't go back.

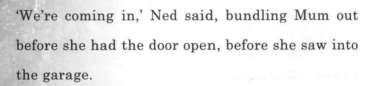

It was agreed we'd be home-schooled. We read and wrote with Mum. Dad did maths with us when he wasn't too tired. Grandad's job was to teach us geography and history. He mainly told us stories.

'Right then, I want to hear you both read then you're off to Grandad's,' Mum said.

Ned led Mum away and again I had an urge to shout, to call, *Help, Mum. Look at this . . . this thing.* But somehow it was important to Ned, this secret. Before the world saw Leonard, I needed to find out why.

I shoved the urge back down and followed them. I turned the tap off and shut the door, sliding the latch across. No one but us entered the garage any more.

Inside the house, Ned picked a book off the shelf about sea creatures – one that Grandad had given us when Mum first pulled us out of school. I raised an eyebrow at my brother. He grinned.

Mum raised both eyebrows. 'I thought you were reading that Tyke Tyler book. The man in the bookshop said it was really good.'

'Finished it,' Ned replied. 'It was good. *Really good*.'

He hadn't finished it. His bookmark had moved only a few pages a day.

'Where is it?' Mum asked.

Ned and I both knew why she wanted it. She liked to ask us questions. She quizzed us on what we read. If we got less than seven out of ten we had to read the book again.

'Erm,' Ned replied. 'I think I left it at Grandad's.'

Mum opened her mouth to speak.

Ned interrupted her. 'Yeah, I definitely left it at Grandad's. Didn't I, Jamie?'

I nodded but couldn't hold back a smile.

Mum narrowed her eyes at me like I was the culprit. 'You can read to me first then, Jamie. What are you reading?'

I read to Mum about a boy called Billy and a fox cub running away from home. Ned flicked through the sea creatures book.

When it was his turn to read aloud, I abandoned Billy's adventures and listened as my brother read about wolffish.

'*Fearsome in looks, the wolffish is also known as the devil fish. Its strong, wide jaw and sharp teeth that give the fish its name are used to crush hard-shell molluscs and crustaceans. Despite its reputation as a bottom-feeder . . .*'

Ned stopped reading and grinned at me. We laughed. *Bottom-feeder.*

Mum growled, 'Get on with it.'

'. . . *the wolffish is not small, growing up to five foot in length. This shy creature lives on the ocean floor in rocky nooks and small caves . . .*'

'Look at it . . .' Ned said, holding the book up to me as we walked towards Grandad's, just a few streets away. You could only see the sea from Grandad's top windows. 'It looks like Leonard, right?'

There was something in the wide mouth, something in the jaw. And the fin that ran the length of the fish's back was identical to those that ran in rows down Leonard's head. Leonard wasn't a wolffish, but he wasn't a wolffish like Ned and I weren't monkeys. Distant relations.

'We should show it to Grandad,' I said.

Ned frowned at me.

'We should show Leonard to Grandad,' I tried again.

Ned thought for a moment. Then shook his head. 'They'll take it away like they did with E.T.' He had made Dad take us to see *E.T. the Extra-Terrestrial* three times at the cinema. It was his favourite film after the *Star Trek* ones.

But later, after lunch of potted shrimp on toast, I couldn't help but say, 'Have you ever heard of people living in the sea, Grandad?'

'Of course, Jamie. Lots of people live their lives in boats. In 1963, I only spent three days on dry land.'

We knew this story. Grandad had crewed a ship called the *Dublin*. The crew called it *Great White*. They'd made their money ferrying spices. Grandad said a crate of saffron could buy a small house. And a little crate at that.

'No, I mean, *in the sea.*'

Ned coughed. Not a real one at first, but it

became a fit, hacking and hacking till he spat into his handkerchief.

'All right, Captain?' Grandad said to Ned. My brother nodded and Grandad turned to me. 'You mean mermaids.'

So instead of a lesson, Grandad told us the stories he could remember about mermaids. Explorers' stories. Pirates' stories. Myths and legends. The mermaids were usually beautiful. Mostly the head and torso of a woman and the tail of a fish, rising from the water, enchanting men.

Nothing like Leonard.

'Do they always look like that?' I asked.

'In the stories,' Ned added.

'Not always,' Grandad said. 'We heard a good story in the war . . .

'*A Japanese ship, posted to Indonesia, found itself in calm water, off a small, unfamiliar island.*

The captain, an old seadog, had suffered from a heart attack on the voyage. He'd survived it but was quite happy to wait there for orders.

'They waited for days, the crew restless, the captain bedbound and growing weaker by the day. As they waited, they saw things in the water, things no one had seen before. The captain wouldn't believe his crew's stories, till he hauled himself from his sick bed and saw for himself.

'He peered into the depths, groaning from his aching body and they surfaced in the water all around the boat. Merpeople! These weren't like the mermaids in legends. They were more like tiny humans. About yay high.' Grandad held out his hand, two feet off the ground. *'They had limbs like*

you and I, but a mouth like a carp and spiked fins on their heads.'

I gasped, not a loud dramatic gasp, just a short sucking of air. Ned made a 'hmm' noise.

Grandad continued. 'The creatures stayed with the ship for days on end while the water was calm and no orders came. The captain was enchanted and seemed to be returning to health. An artist in a previous life, he spent hours trying again and again to draw them.

'The ship had been at anchor for over a week when, one night, the captain disappeared. His drawings went with him and the mysterious creatures were not seen again. Had the mer taken the captain? Had he gone willingly? Nobody knew. Nobody

35

had been on deck to see him. The captain had sent the night-watchman to his bunk under a strict command not to come back to his post that night.

'The next day, orders came to return to port. The crew took the ship and their story back home.'

Grandad looked at us. Our eyes were wide. Our mouths hung open.

'That story slivered like an eel from ship to ship. I don't think the Japanese liked the laughter. The first mate and half the crew were tried for mutiny. Their commanders believed they had killed the captain and flung him overboard. The crew stuck to their story, though. Even when they stood on the firing line.

'But if there *were* mermaids out there,' Grandad finished, 'I'd have seen 'em. Not a drop of ocean I haven't been in.'

I looked at Ned. Ned stared at me.

'What if there were, Grandad?' I said at the same time as my brother blurted, 'I need to talk to you, Jamie.'

Grandad shook his head. 'You boys are in a funny mood today. I'm going to make some tea. You work it out.'

When Grandad had left, my brother, usually all smiles and laughter, looked at me seriously.

'Jamie, I don't want to tell him.'

'We've got to. What if it's dangerous?'

Ned scratched his head just behind his ear. 'What does that matter any more?' he said.

I had no answer for this. I shrugged and frowned.

'Everything's going, Jamie. This, this –' Ned pointed to his chest, to where his lungs were filling with rubbish – 'is taking everything. Everything. Soon.'

37

We stared at each other. My lips hardened. I scrubbed a hand across my eyes.

Ned had no fear of his future. He said, 'If this is our last adventure, I want it to be *just* ours.'

Leonard

People always assume Ned's my little brother. He is almost a foot shorter than me. Where I'm broad like Dad, Ned's tiny. He could pass for a six-year-old. He's eleven. We're both eleven.

Ned *is* my little brother, but only by eight minutes.

Mum and Dad say he came into the world coughing and he hasn't stopped since. You expect twins to have the same lives, do all the same things. Ned and I had different lives from the start; they rushed him away to clear all the gunk from his lungs while I slept peacefully swaddled.

It wasn't till later that they knew what his

condition was. Mum said she took him to the doctor because he tasted salty. The doctor knew what was wrong straightaway.

It was the first time any of us had heard the words *cystic fibrosis*. We're experts now.

When we got back from Grandad's, Mum made Ned have a rest. A rest meant lying on the sofa, re-watching *Star Trek*. My brother gave me a look as he sat down and I stood by the door.

'You not going to sit with your brother, Jamie?' Mum said.

'Erm,' I replied. On the way home, I'd agreed on the secret, on our adventure – and we'd agreed that if we were keeping Leonard, then he needed feeding.

Although our lives were very different we usually stuck together. When they took Ned out of school, Mum had wanted me to stay there. But I ran for the school gates and away home every day. I had this terrible feeling that I'd lose him, that he'd go and I wouldn't get a chance to say goodbye.

After a week of the same, my teacher and my parents agreed it would be best if I was home-schooled too.

'Erm,' I said again. I could not think of a reason why I wasn't watching *Star Trek*.

Ned rescued me. 'He's got to put the bikes away. Haven't you, Jamie? We just left them by the gate *like the lazy dogs that we are*.' He laughed, the moment of seriousness forgotten.

Mum frowned.

I slipped away.

I leaned the bikes by the garage door. The latch had not been touched. I slid it across, pushed open the door, just a touch, and peered inside. The light was off but I could see the lip of the tub in the gloom. I opened the door a little more and reached for the light switch. I flicked it on. Nothing happened. I flicked again. Nothing. I opened the door wide and looked up at the bulb. It was smashed.

I pulled the door shut with me on the outside. I thought about the wolffish, living in the dark depths of the ocean, and I made a note: Leonard doesn't like light.

I needed light, though. I knew where my torch was and fetched it from our bedroom. But before I went back to the garage, I snuck down to the cellar and the deep freeze.

We never get through all the fish that Grandad gives us – Dad isn't a huge fan of fish. So I took a plastic bag of frozen herring out of the freezer and tried to creep back to Leonard.

'What you doing, Jamie?' Mum called from the kitchen.

I had planned my answer this time. 'Ned got a puncture. Just fixing it.'

'Yeah, I did, Mum,' Ned shouted over the sound of phasers shooting down an enemy spaceship.

There was no sign of Leonard in the tub. I shone the torch into every corner of the garage but still nothing.

'Hello,' I said.

No answer.

I pulled open the bag and threw one frozen herring towards the bath. It hit the edge with a crack then slid into the water. I shone the torch towards it as it bobbed on the surface.

Ned would have strolled in and peered into the tub. He was the brave one. In *Star Trek*, he would have been Captain Kirk. I would have been the doctor, Leonard McCoy. McCoy was the cautious one.

'*Damn it, Jim, I'm a doctor not a merman keeper,*' Bones would say.

No away mission takes place without Kirk and now I was stuck without Ned. Like when you stand just beyond the waves' wash and let your feet sink into the wet sand.

I imagined my brother beside me. 'Boldly go,' I whispered, and took one step, still watching the herring.

A scuttle. A scurry. A splash. And Leonard was back in the tub, returned from his hiding place. A hand shot out of the water. It was just a flash and the herring was gone. Ripples spread out across the bath from where the fish had been.

I nearly dropped the torch.

I couldn't go any further. I needed Captain Kirk ahead of me. I threw two more herring into the bath, then I dropped the empty bag and ran.

Outside, I made sure the latch was all the way across before leaning against the closed door and gulping in air.

Ned was asleep when I got back. Mum had wrapped a blanket around him. Spock was warning Captain Kirk against fighting an alien with his bare hands. Kirk was ignoring him.

'Right, Jamie, I want to get some writing out of you,' Mum said.

We didn't make it back to the garage that afternoon. Ned slept the rest of the day while I wrote about the storm. Dad got home early and filthy. He was always filthy. But he set me some maths before his bath.

When Ned woke, it was dinner time. Then the rain came. Big heavy drops – the kind of rain we knew Mum would never let Ned out in.

'You boys have a good day?' Dad asked. He drank coffee. We had mugs of hot chocolate.

'Yeah,' Ned said. 'You can't beat a big sleep.'

'Did you get anything good on the beach, though?' Sometimes Dad came treasure hunting with us at the weekends.

'Erm . . .' I said, pushing down the urge to shout once more.

'Just a shoe,' Ned finished.

We all agreed that was pretty rubbish. We had too many shoes. Dad knew a man who collected abandoned buckets and spades and hung them off a tree in his front garden. We had enough shoes for a shoe tree.

'Mum wouldn't like that though,' Dad said.

'We could . . . *persuade her*,' Ned said with a grin.

'Maybe one day.' Dad winked.

In our bunks, Ned on the top, me on the bottom, I told Ned about the herring. He wasn't surprised.

'That's what mermen must eat,' he said. 'We should get him some mussels too. I reckon Leonard loves mussels.'

That was the first time I felt it. Not jealousy yet. Just a strange feeling that something was happening, something unknowable, between my brother and the fish-man living in our garage.

Song

One of Grandad's favourite stories was one about the night he heard the whales sing. He'd been at sea for weeks. It's not easy for sailors to get lost. Unless it's cloudy, then the stars are hidden at night and the sun is gone for most of the day. Before the whales sang, the ship's equipment had broken and the clouds had been thick for three days and nights.

'That's the only time I've ever been truly scared at sea,' Grandad would say. *'If a storm had come, we would not have had the foggiest where shallow water or rocks might be.'*

They put the ship at anchor and slept, praying for clear skies in the morning.

'That night every soul on board was woken by deep singing. You can hear history in a whale's song – each booming note slowly shaking your bones, vibrating through you. We all went out on deck and there they were. Huge beasts, shining in the moonlight. A gam of whales.'

Grandad said that the captain, Long Ben, was one of the best seamen he'd ever known. 'Knew the sea like a mother.'

Long Ben called for the anchor to be raised. The crew fired up the engine and followed the whales. And when the sun rose, they were in sight of land and in the shipping lane they'd lost. With a song, the whales had led them home.

The night after we found Leonard, I couldn't sleep; there was a whistle on the wind. Leonard was singing.

'Jamie,' Ned said. 'Can you hear him?'

We stared out of our window, down to the garage and across the sea. Leonard's home was somewhere out there. Maybe Leonard had a family waiting for him to come home. Maybe he was lost.

'Ned,' I whispered, and for the first time I said what we both knew. 'We can't keep him for ever.'

Ned wasn't listening. He was searching for something in his drawer. He came back to the window with his Walkman. Dad had bought it last time my brother had a long stay in hospital. It was the one with the big microphone unit on the top. Our friend Tibs, who lived at the post office round the corner, had been so jealous when he had seen it.

Ned pushed open the window, but before pressing record he turned back to me. 'You can't keep anything for ever,' he whispered.

Appointment

The next day was one Ned wanted to get away from. Mum and Dad had learned not to tell him when those days were coming. Otherwise he'd be gone before morning and we'd spend the day searching for him.

The last time that happened, Mum had been distraught. She thought we'd lost Ned for good, till I found him rock-pooling on the cliffs by Portland Bill.

Now Mum just wakes us from the doorway with her tea in hand and her dressing gown wrapped round her and says, 'Appointment today, Neddy. Dad's waiting downstairs.' And Dad would be waiting in the hallway. No chance of Ned slipping away.

Ned usually swears when he hears this news. That day he didn't say anything.

'You all right, Ned?' Mum said.

I grabbed his bunk and pulled myself up to peer at him. 'He's not there, Mum,' I said.

Mum swore. 'How did he know?' she said, then shouted to Dad, 'Did you tell him, Charlie?'

'What?' Dad called back.

'He's not here.'

'Where is he, Jamie?' Dad yelled.

I was always expected to know. Like I was expected to make sure Ned didn't do too much. Get him home on time. Keep *our* room tidy. Even my parents forgot we were the same age.

I did have a good idea where he was this time, though. 'I'll check the garage,' I said before anyone else thought of it.

'Ned,' I whispered as the door squeaked open.

There was a splash, then a torch flicked on. The beam was directed at me. 'Ned?' I said again.

'Shhh,' my brother whispered. 'He doesn't like noise.' He flicked the torch off again. 'Or light.'

I stayed by the open door. I could see my brother, just a dark outline in the few beams of light I let into the garage. 'Did you talk to him?' I said.

Ned laughed quietly. 'Do you think Leonard speaks English?' he asked. 'I just *know*. Talking's not the word exactly.'

I stood and stared. I did not know what to make of Ned's knowing. It felt like *our adventure* was fast becoming Ned's adventure. Jealousy crawled across my skin.

'He touched me,' my brother said. 'When I coughed, he touched me here.' I could see my brother's hand pressed against his chest. 'His hand is so cold.'

I'd heard a doctor whisper the word 'hopeless' to my parents at Ned's last appointment. Maybe doctors didn't know everything. Maybe Leonard was more than just a fish-man. In stories, strange creatures brought about strange events. Magical events. Did Leonard have any magic in his fingertips?

I told Ned about his appointment. He swore then, still whispering. He asked me to help him escape.

'You've got to go, Ned,' I said. 'It might be different this time.'

I heard Ned grunt in the dark, then whisper again, maybe to me, maybe to Leonard, 'And they might give me the moon on a stick.'

Superstition

We went to London once. Mum says everyone should visit the capital even if it does take hours and hours crammed in Dad's van. When we were there, she wanted us to go to all the museums and see dinosaur bones and paintings of old ladies. Dad just wanted to take photos of all the buildings made of Portland stone, cathedrals and banks and galleries. Even a palace. Ned said that the island must be almost hollow seeing as how so much of it is in London.

Portland is like the holey cheese Mum gets when it's on special offer. The one with the red wax. It's full of holes. On Portland, if your dad's not a fisherman, he's a quarryman. Apart from

Tibs' dad, who runs the post office. And Lucy and Peewee's. He's a policeman. *The* policeman. Officer Taylor.

Before a rockfall in the quarries, or a cave-in, rabbits escape the burrows. You can't say 'rabbit' on Portland. It's bad luck. Grandad says it's silly superstition and Dad calls it the 'R-word', like it's a swear word. Ned loves to say it.

Grandad does have his own superstitions. He tells us myths and legends and stories of why the world is the way it is. Sometimes I think he belongs to another age, one before cars and Walkmans and *Star Trek*. And I guess, like all old people, he does.

Ned had left with Mum and Dad, growling, 'Let's get the hell out of here,' before stomping through the door. Grandad came by a little later.

When I'd fixed his tea and we were sitting at the kitchen table he said, 'You got me thinking, Jamie. About mermaids.'

He asked me if I remembered when we studied stars. Grandad's stories often started like this. I didn't wonder what stars had to do with mermaids. I knew we'd get there.

In the summer, when we learned about stars, Grandad took us out at night to look at them – we didn't need to go beyond our back garden. He taught us how the Earth and the other planets moved, and we found Venus in the sky and the North Star and a host of constellations.

I told Grandad I remembered.

'You know all the constellations we *can* see,' Grandad said.

I did know. I also knew what Grandad told me next, that there are lots of constellations we can't see. They only appear in the southern half of the sky. People who see them can't see our constellations. Orion never fires his bow across their sky.

Grandad took a sip of tea, then continued, 'There's one called *Piscis Austrinus* – the southern fish. It peeks into our northern sky in autumn and winter. You can see just one star: a very important star if you want to find your way, Fomalhaut. *Fum al-hut* means the "mouth of the fish". It's Arabic.'

Grandad told me to get him paper and pencil. 'Get your atlas too,' he called.

Back at the table, he made seven big dots. He joined them up with bold, straight lines to make the outline of a fish. '*Piscis Austrinus,*' he said. 'Very old constellation. The Greeks knew it. And the Egyptians. Goes all the way back to Babylonia, though.' He reached for the atlas and flicked through the pages. 'Here,' Grandad said, and placed the thick book down in front of us. 'Right, that's Iraq here' – he traced the outline of a country with his finger – 'and Syria there.' He traced another country. 'This is where the Babylonian empire was. They had lots of gods, the Babylonians. One chief one was Atargatis. You got that?'

I nodded at Grandad and mouthed, 'At-ar-ga-tis.'

'Atargatis was the mistress of her people. She was responsible for their protection, making sure they were well and healthy and prosperous.

'But one day she did something no god is allowed to do. She fell in love. With a young man. The goddess took him

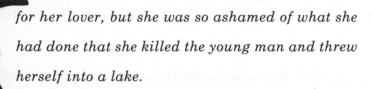

for her lover, but she was so ashamed of what she had done that she killed the young man and threw herself into a lake.

'Of course, being a god, she didn't die but became half-fish, half-lady. And she continued to protect her people from the deep. She protected them against calamities and hardship. She and her many children protected them against illness too.'

I thought about Leonard's cold touch. I thought about Ned's cough. I wondered if the children of Atargatis were still in the business of protecting. Would that protection extend to miracles? That's what we needed: a miracle – nothing less. Maybe it would come at the touch of our strange friend.

'They named those stars in her honour. The Great Fish, they called them. And when they saw Fomalhaut rise, they'd know she was still watching over them.

'And that, Jamie, is the story of the first mermaid.'

Grandad had finished his tea. He put his hand up to my head. 'You all right there?' he said. 'Looking a bit pale.'

'I'm OK,' I said. 'That's just a good story.'

Grandad said, 'Ned'll be all right,' even though he didn't know that. I nodded and suggested we leave mermaids for a while and look at the atlas. We stayed in Iraq and Syria, travelled down through Jordan, then into Israel. When we hit the Mediterranean Sea, Grandad proposed we have a little rest before lunch. I made him another tea and sat in the front room.

I couldn't settle, though. My head was full of mermaids and mermen, protecting people, making sure they were well. My head was full of the children of Atargatis.

I thought I didn't mind if our adventure became Ned's adventure if it led to something good. If it led to a miracle, this child of Atargatis – Leonard – could have my brother to himself.

Right then, I believed a miracle was coming.

Fear

When you're home-schooled you don't have many friends. You have to be friends with other mums who come over for tea and biscuits. And policemen who live three doors down. And fishermen whose names you don't know. We've made friends with our postman, Bill, who's a big *Star Trek* fan too. He bought Ned a Starfleet badge when he found out Ned was ill. We have friends up and down our little road.

Mrs Clarke next door isn't amongst them. Dad calls her 'a nosy old bat'. Tony, the policeman, says she phones the station about all sorts of tiny things. Mum says we need to look after her, she's very old. But I heard Mum calling her 'cow,' under

her breath when she came to complain that Mum was hoovering too loudly.

Ned and I still have one friend from school. Tibs. On the day Ned was at his appointment, when Grandad finished my lessons and closed his eyes for a nap, I went to check on Leonard and Tibs found me there, with my ear pressed against the garage door. He called from the front gate where he sat on his bike.

Tibs had vomited the night before. He hadn't told his mum he'd snuck a whole packet of mint Viscounts from the cupboard and eaten half of them before dinner, so she thought he was ill and wouldn't let him go to school. But she'd seen he was 'recovered' soon after breakfast and told him to get out from under her feet.

'Go see Ned and Jamie.'

'So here I am,' Tibs said. 'Where's Ned?'

'Hospital.'

'He all right?'

I shrugged at this. I didn't say anything about the miracle I hoped for.

Tibs went red for a moment, then said, 'So, do you want to go to the prison or something?'

The prison sits on the highest hill on Portland. The road winds up and up. You can see the beach behind you all the way. We don't go there for the prison or for the views. We go there for the ride back down. We call it *the Slalom* and shout the theme tune to *Ski Sunday* as we pedal.

If you go too fast you skid off on the bends. You haven't gone fast enough if you don't lose your bike a few times.

Last time Ned went up, he came home with both his knees dripping blood and his right eyebrow split open. Ned is fearless. He's banned from the prison road now.

I agreed to go with Tibs. I couldn't stand and listen by the closed garage door all morning. And I couldn't go in. No Kirk to go before me.

I went to check with Grandad. He was asleep. I was pretty sure he'd be fine with me going, though. I fetched my bike from beside the garage and checked the latch. It was as far across as it could be.

I turned away from Tibs, who was waiting by the gate, and whispered through the door, 'I'll bring some more fish later.' I would, when Ned was back. Then I remembered my brother laughing at me. Leonard can't speak English.

As we mounted our bikes outside the gate,

Mrs Clarke appeared, a broom in one hand and a cigarette in the other. 'Shouldn't you boys be learning something somewhere?' she called.

It was usually Ned who spoke for us when needed. I tried to think what my brother would say.

'We're going on a field trip, Mrs Clarke,' was the best I could come up with.

As we cycled away, little Peter, Peewee, waved from his front garden and shouted at us, 'Hello!'

We waved back.

Tibs is fast going downhill but slow on the way up. He spends his Saturdays in the post office selling stamps and nicking sweets off his dad's shelves. He's a bit rounder than most of the boys at school.

'Slow down, Jamie,' he called to me as I pedalled away up the hill.

I was used to waiting. Ned was getting weaker all the time. I remember when we were little, apart from the cough and all the doctors, there wasn't much between me and my twin. He'd stopped growing, though, while I'd shot up taller than Mum.

We went as high as we could, all the way to the *No Entry for Unauthorised Personnel* sign. We stopped and stared down at Portland, the beach and the coast of the mainland spread out before us.

'So, how is Ned?' Tibs asked.

At school, some time before we'd left, they'd had this assembly about considering people's differences and not asking about things you did not understand. Everyone knew it was about Ned. People weren't supposed to ask how he was.

Ned didn't like it. He'd rather just tell people to shut their mouths, whenever they asked.

That instruction made me happy though, because people asked me more than they asked Ned. I had nothing to tell them; no one talked to me about the illness.

I had nothing to tell Tibs now, nothing that wasn't about a fish-man, living in our garage. I shrugged. 'Let's go,' I said, and set off fast. I soon slowed. I was Leonard McCoy. I didn't go anywhere boldly.

'Damn it, Jim. I'm a doctor not a stunt cyclist.'

Risk

Grandad was pleased I'd gone out with Tibs. He worried about us being cooped up too much. He had argued with Mum and Dad when they took us out of school. As Ned grew weaker though, so did Grandad's arguments. Now he wanted my brother *in* as much as our parents did. He still wanted me *out*, though.

Grandad and I had cheese on toast for lunch. Grandad ate his with a raw onion. I had mine with tomato. Then we played Risk.

Grandad says you can learn a lot of history and geography from *Risk: The World Conquest Game*. You have a map of the world split into territories, not all real countries, then you have your own little army and have to conquer the world.

In Grandad's version, you can't conquer a territory unless you can answer a question about it. If you want to conquer Western Australia you might need to know that Willem Janszoon was the first European to see its coastline. Or that Australia was called New Holland when it was first discovered. If you want to conquer the Urals you'd need to know that their highest point is Mount Narodnaya or, an easier one, that they form the border between Europe and Asia. If you wanted Argentina, you'd need to know why we had just been at war over the Falkland Islands, that British settlers had landed there in 1690 or that the Falklands had been under British rule for one hundred and fifty years.

Risk is a long game. Usually no one wins. Grandad says that's like real war, another important lesson.

I thought I had the upper hand when Ned and my parents got home. I had secured South and North America, and I had begun an invasion across Africa but had to stop when I couldn't tell Grandad how many men had defended Rorke's Drift against four thousand Zulu warriors. One hundred and fifty, he told me. We shared Europe and Asia. Grandad only had full control of Australia, the smallest of the continents.

'Nice work,' Ned said, looking over my shoulder at the board.

Ned was no good at Risk. He often said things like, 'Why do I need to know that the official languages of Canada are English and French? I'm never gonna go there.' He never made defences either. Grandad called him 'Kamikaze Ned'.

Kamikaze is a kind of suicide attack. In the war, Japanese pilots would fly explosive laden planes into Allied ships. That's where the word comes from.

And that's how Ned played. He risked everything. That was the name of the game, Risk, but it wasn't a tactic that paid off.

Risk was Ned's tactic for life too – adventures far from home, adopting strange creatures, boldly going where I feared to go – and he seemed to enjoy it as much as he enjoyed sending his little plastic troops on a suicidal attack.

Mum hadn't come into the kitchen. She was crying in the hallway. Dad was pretending to make tea but I could tell he was listening to Mum too.

'How was it?' I said to Dad.

He shook his head, which either meant 'Not good' or 'Don't ask' or a combination of both. Mum was still crying and Grandad was listening now.

'Boys, can you go out for a minute? Anything you can do outside?' Dad said.

Maybe risk wasn't a tactic that paid off in life either. We'd brought risk home from the beach. We kept it locked up in our garage. Risk was worth it if it led to that miracle. But one thing was clear – a miracle had not arrived.

The hospital appointments were never good. What Ned had, people don't get better from. They take pills and medicines which sometimes make the symptoms, like his cough, better or sometimes don't. But the people never get better. They only get worse.

Before they stopped taking me along on appointments, I remember a doctor saying some people beat the odds. Some people with Ned's condition live a long time. But the doctors didn't think my brother was going to be one of them.

Outside, I asked Ned, 'How was it?'

He shrugged and pulled a face. 'You know,' he said, shrugging at me like I'd shrugged at Tibs. Then he asked, 'How's Leonard?'

My brother was cross that I hadn't been to see *our little fishy friend*.

'He'll be lonely,' Ned said. 'And starving.'

I didn't tell Ned about my fear of Leonard. My brother didn't understand fear. I just shrugged back; Leonard's hunger held a small place in my mind compared to Ned's hospital appointment.

We couldn't go back inside to the freezer yet.

'Mussels?' I suggested.

'Yes!' Ned said.

I picked up my bike while Ned bent over and coughed. 'You stay here.' I promised to be back in twenty minutes with some mussels. They're

easy to find if you know where to look. I pedalled furiously and thought about Ned's cough and Mum's tears and the shake of Dad's head.

The first time they'd left me at home, instead of taking me along to the hospital, I'd muttered, 'That's so unfair.'

Mum had gasped.

Dad had got pretty angry, pretty quickly. 'Jamie,' he'd said. 'Don't you ever talk about what's fair and what's not.'

But I knew it was all unfair. It was unfair for all of us.

I couldn't ask anyone what they'd said at the hospital. It was unfair that I was the only one not to know. But I couldn't say that either.

Injury

Often in *Star Trek*, when the crew encounter alien life there are some side effects: the whole crew lose their minds and start prancing around on some distant planet; someone gets psychic powers; Sulu, the ship's pilot, thinks he's a pirate. That kind of thing. If they met someone like our Leonard, the other Leonard – the *Enterprise*'s doctor – would want to be sure he wasn't poisonous to them or they weren't poisonous to him.

We had no idea what effect our Leonard would have on us. Like Captain Kirk, Ned had no caution though.

When I got back from the beach, I had

a pocket full of grey-black mussels. I pushed open the squeaking door and heard the same splash from the morning. Ned was back where he had been, perched on the edge of the tub.

'Come in,' he whispered.

'Is he safe?' I whispered back.

'Of course he is.'

I still went slowly, cautiously, and stopped a few steps back. When my eyes had adjusted to the gloom, I could see him. Beneath the surface. Peering up at us. His eyes were huge – big globes, goggling out of his head.

'Did you get the mussels?'

I fished a few from my pocket and held them out. Ned took them and dropped them into the tub away from the spot where bubbles were rising from Leonard's gills.

The merman's left arm shot out and grabbed

one. He put it straight in to his mouth. I could see big, sharp teeth like the wolffish. He crunched through the shell and it was gone.

'More?' Ned said. 'I knew he'd love mussels.'

I handed them over, three at a time. Leonard ate them all in the same way. His left hand grabbed, his jaws crushed.

'I think he's hurt.' My brother pointed towards the fish-man's right arm. It hadn't moved and hung at his side.

'Yeah, you're right. Looks like Dad's did,' I said.

Ned nodded.

Dad got hurt at work a lot. Grandad said the injuries were the only thing that made working at a quarry like being a seaman. Dad had broken some bones, torn muscles and cut his head open. Once he came home with a dislocated shoulder.

'It'll just pop back in,' he'd said. It didn't. He lay around for a day and a night, wincing and drinking tea until Mum made him go to the doctor.

Leonard's shoulder looked the same, floppy and dead, like one of the eels Grandad hung in his shed to smoke.

Leonard had finished his meal. He stared at us, like we stared at him. No one spoke. After several minutes, the merman bobbed to the surface. His legs were bent like a frog's, ready to spring.

I spoke in the slightest whisper. I told Ned the story of Atargatis, the first mermaid.

'Her job was to protect her people?' Ned said.

I nodded, still staring down at Leonard.

'Like *Doctor Who*?'

I nodded again. 'I thought, Ned, maybe he's here for you?'

Ned frowned at this, frowned and chewed his

lip. He opened his mouth to reply but a cough took him instead. He tried to quiet it and spluttered through his hands.

Leonard did not have eyebrows. He couldn't frown, but his forehead and the spiked frills across his skull pulled downwards and his lips tightened when he heard that coughing. He moved towards Ned, quick as a fish and rose out of the water, kicking upwards. He rested a hand on Ned's knee and pressed his head to my brother's chest.

'Oh, rabbits,' Ned said.

'See, he knows, about you. Maybe he will . . .' I couldn't say it.

We stayed completely still till we heard Mum calling, 'Boys!'

Another splash and Leonard was gone, back below the surface. Ned and I scrambled to our feet and out of the door.

'Dinner,' Mum said from the back door.

We nodded and said we'd be right in.

I slid the latch across as Ned said, 'We'll fix him up. Make him better. But, Jamie, I don't think—'

'Boys!' Mum called again.

I spent dinner thinking about how to ask Dad about his dislocated shoulder. I didn't need to bother.

When Mum slid bowls of Ned's favourite dessert, apple crumble, in front of us, my brother said, 'How did the doctor fix your dislocated shoulder, Dad?'

'What?' Dad said.

'You're such a funny boy, Neddy,' Grandad chuckled.

Dad told us the doctor just kind of rolled it

round and round. He showed us by twirling his arm. He knocked his tea over and Mum called him a lummox.

'Then it just popped back in. Very painful,' Dad said. 'They gave me lots of painkillers and strapped it up after. Still a bit gammy.'

'Painkillers and strapped it up,' Ned repeated.

Mum glared at us. 'You boys won't be doing anything that might dislocate a shoulder, though. I'm not having you go anywhere for a while, not till . . .' After she said 'till', Mum put her hand to her mouth like she was trying to force the words back in. Then she started crying again.

'Come on, love,' Dad said.

'Let's finish our game of Risk,' Grandad said. 'I've moved the board through.'

In the front room, Ned joined Grandad's team. I continued my assault on Africa. Ned's attacks were as suicidal as usual. He punctured my defence in North America by crossing the Bering Strait from Russia and knowing that Alaska is the biggest state in the USA. An easy question. He spread himself too thin, though. After I'd conquered Africa (*Nelson Mandela is imprisoned on Robben Island*), I smashed back through and took Asia in three goes (*Japan surrendered at the end of World War II after two cities were destroyed by atomic bombs – Hiroshima and Nagasaki*).

We all agreed I'd won.

Mum hadn't stopped crying.

Later, when we were meant to be sleeping, we listened to Leonard singing the song of the sea, of waves and wind and wild currents. We listened to Leonard singing and Mum and Dad talking. If they could hear anything but themselves, their fears and worries, they'd have heard him too. They'd have heard him but not known what could make that wild whistling call.

'What are we gonna do?' Mum said.

Dad didn't answer. We'd never seen Dad cry but I thought I heard a whimper then.

There was a whimper and a sob and the whistling song of our merman.

We listened some more and then, 'Jamie,' Ned said, 'I think you're right. I think he's here for a reason.'

Of course, I'd been thinking the same, thinking it wasn't chance that led us to that patch of seaweed. But hope is a fragile thing and my hope was sinking fast. So I just said, 'Maybe. Like in the stories. Like Atargatis. Like the Japanese captain.'

There was silence for a moment. No tears

from downstairs. Then Ned said, 'But he didn't get better, did he – the Japanese captain?'

I didn't want to think about this. Instead, I said, 'We can't keep him in the shed for ever.'

'He can share the bottom bunk with you.' My brother laughed.

We both laughed, just a brief *ha*.

'I don't want to let him go,' Ned said quietly, while I thought the same.

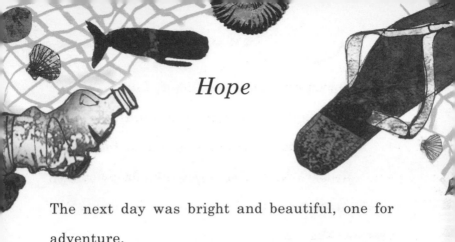

Hope

The next day was bright and beautiful, one for adventure.

'Can we go out?' Ned asked.

Mum's reply was simple. She didn't even look up from the porridge. 'No.'

'Come on, Mum,' my brother tried again. 'You can't just keep us locked up here for ever.'

It occurred to me for a moment that I wasn't locked up, that I could go out, go to school, ride the Slalom with Tibs, go crabbing on the quayside with Lucy. But I wouldn't, couldn't leave Ned. You don't abandon your captain. That's mutiny.

I didn't say any of this.

Mum swirled round. The wooden spoon was

still in her hand. Globs of porridge sprayed across the table and across our bowls and our T-shirts.

'I can and I will. I'm not having you get sick.'

Neither of us dared reply. We looked down at the splattered table. As Mum turned back to the porridge, Ned whispered, not for me, just for himself, 'But I *am* sick.'

I got a cloth and cleared up the mess.

After breakfast, Ned had to try some new medicine that the doctor had given him the day before. Mum calmed a little.

'You can go in the garden,' she said. 'But don't even think about opening that front gate.'

Leonard wasn't in his tub. He was sitting on a cardboard box full of shoes, holding something, inspecting it.

We'd snuck some herring out. Ned waved

one at him and said, 'Leonard.' He didn't move, just glanced up at us then opened his mouth. His tongue made a few quiet clicking noises.

'What have you got, Len?' Ned said, and crept towards him.

I stayed by the empty tub. 'Careful, Ned.'

Leonard looked up at Ned, at me, back to my twin. He flattened out his hand to show the bone whale that had sat on a high shelf – one of the prizes of our collection.

'That's good, isn't it?' Ned whispered.

Leonard made some more clicking noises.

'Yeah, you can have it.' Ned pointed at the whale, pointed at Leonard.

The merman's smile didn't look much like a human smile. His eyes widened. His lips thinned. He showed his big teeth. He clutched the carved whale tightly.

We hadn't seen him walk before. His legs bent the wrong way, like a frog's. His walk was bouncier than ours, like he was Neil Armstrong, walking on the moon.

When he was back in the water, he put the bone whale on the bottom of the tub and reached for the herring that Ned still held.

'Do you think he's a boy?' my brother whispered. 'Or a man?'

I didn't answer. I didn't know.

'I've been thinking about Long Ben's wife,' Ned said.

'What?'

'Long Ben, Grandad's old captain.'

'I know who Long Ben is,' I said.

'And his wife, lost at sea. Maybe she saw the mer, like the Japanese captain.'

'She was sick too,' I said.

We watched Leonard eat and thought about why he had come.

Long Ben had never married. He'd been at sea all his life. He'd lied about his age and joined the Navy just before war began. He was fourteen.

He didn't even know how to speak to the women that came to dance with the sailors whenever they were on shore leave. For his whole seventeenth year, he didn't even see a woman – his ship was blown to pieces and he spent fourteen months in Italy as a prisoner of war.

When the war ended, he stayed at sea. He didn't know he was missing something. When his crew left the ship at various ports around the world to see wives and girlfriends, he'd stay with his only lady, the sea.

Then one day, unloading their ship in Manila, everything changed for Long Ben. He met a woman called Perla and fell deeply in love. He gave up his ship and the sea and stayed right there. Grandad, as first mate, had to take on the captaincy and get them all back home, where the crew broke up and went their separate ways.

A long time later, Grandad had run into his old captain, not far away from Portland, in the little village of Lulworth.

Long Ben told Grandad that he and Perla had many happy years together. They'd lived a simple life just outside Manila. The seaman didn't even miss the sea. But one day Perla got sick, then sicker. It wasn't long before the doctors said she only had a short time to live.

Ben came up with plans to go to different doctors, travel to Europe and America and make Perla better. But Perla had a different plan. She told Long Ben that she just wanted to see the things he'd seen. She wanted to go to sea. She'd heard all his stories and now she wanted to see it for herself. They sold everything, bought a boat and set sail.

Grandad always says that once you've been at sea, you've got salt water in your veins; you never lose your sea legs. Long Ben took them far and wide, while poor Perla got sicker and sicker. Eventually they found themselves in a beautiful cove on a tiny Pacific island. Ben said he'd never seen a finer sight in all his life.

They put the boat at anchor and went down to the cabin and to bed early; with her illness, Perla was always tired.

Long Ben woke a few hours later to the sound of singing. His wife had gone up on deck. He lay and listened. The song washed over him and as he drifted back to sleep, his wife's voice was joined by another voice and another. The sound of the sea, the lapping of the waves, the wind and the birds. Voices overlapping and entwining. Someone or something clicked a rhythm.

In the morning, Perla was not beside him. She was no longer on deck. There was no sign of where she had gone.

Long Ben said that he had not even wept. He could not think of a better way or a finer place for her to say goodbye. Long Ben thought she'd seen enough and given her husband back to his first love – the sea.

He told Grandad that he still heard her singing. On a clear evening, if he bent his ear to the sea, the wind and waves made that song again.

'What if that was mermaids?' Ned said. 'Singing with Perla. What if they came for Perla like they came for the Japanese captain?'

I looked at Ned. I chewed the inside of my mouth. Hope rose in me again. Leonard was here for Jamie. A magical creature to do magical things.

'And like Atargatis,' my brother went on. 'Protecting her people.'

We looked at Leonard.

'Is that why you're here?' my brother said.

A brief smile flickered on my lips. I wanted

to grab Leonard, to hug him, to thank him for coming, for the miracle I was sure he carried.

Instead, I watched him eat until not a single bone was left. The herrings had completely disappeared. No sign they had ever been there.

Operation

'Do you think Calpol will do?' Ned whispered.

We were meant to be reading, while Mum cleaned. Instead, we were planning our operation to fix Leonard.

I shrugged at my brother. 'If Leonard's a kid, maybe.'

'He *is* little.'

'So?' I said.

'Maybe he won't need something too powerful.'

I shrugged again and looked back down at my book about Billy and his fox.

'I hope you're reading in there,' Mum called from the bathroom.

'Indeed we are, Mother,' Ned called back.

'Less cheek. More reading.'

I read. Billy had to let his fox go in the end. Stories often end with letting something go. Ned flicked through the book of fish.

'Might be poison to him, though,' he whispered after a while.

'What?'

'Calpol might be poison to Leonard.'

We agreed to leave the painkillers. Pinching unwanted fish was one thing, rooting around the medicine cabinet was another. But I said I'd find something to make a sling.

Mum appeared at the door. 'Right, Ned, time for your percussion.'

Ned winked at me as I took my book upstairs. I couldn't read; I hated to hear Mum thumping Ned's chest, hear the gunk he coughed up. I listened to Dad's Specials' cassette on the Walkman.

While I listened to the rock-steady beat, I searched through our stuff, settling on a pair of football socks. I cut them open and tied them together. I thought it would work.

Once she'd finished clearing Ned's lungs, Mum said we could go outside, but not further than the gate. I hid the socks in my pocket.

It was a clear day, bright and fresh. A day where the sky goes on and on, as if for ever, till it hits the sea. A day where if you stare at the place where the sea and sky meet for too long, you forget where one begins and the other ends and you forget which is which and it's just blue and blue and blue.

'Bit nippy, eh,' Ned said as we stared.

We knew why we waited. Neither of us wanted to do the deed. Neither of us wanted to try to wriggle the little fish-man's arm back into the socket. We stood by the back fence and neither of us talked about it. But we knew.

'Look,' I said. 'Big one.' A huge boat slowly held its course across the open sea.

'Fishing?'

'Some big industrial job,' I said.

'Probably that's the kind of thing that hurt our little friend.'

This seemed as good an idea as any. Grandad told us about those big trawlers, ripping up the sea bed.

We stared and I imagined Leonard's underwater home, raked and destroyed. I imagined the storm coming and saw him and his damaged arm, flung back and forth. Then we'd found him on our beach.

'Come on, then,' Ned said. 'Let's get this over with.'

★

Leonard was sitting on the edge of his tub again.
He didn't dive under the water. He knew it
was us.

'Morning, Len,' Ned said.

Leonard clicked and gurgled, holding out the
bone whale.

My brother sat by his friend. I stayed by the
door.

'Len,' Ned said. 'We've got to do something.
I don't think you're gonna like it.'

More clicks. More gurgles.

Ned looked up at me. I stared back. 'You've
gotta hold him, Jamie.'

I shook my head a little. I wasn't squeamish
about fish and flesh, but bones and joints . . . Bile
rose in my throat. I shuddered.

Ned nodded, big nods. 'You've got to.'

I'd only touched Leonard once. Back on the beach when I'd pressed one finger into his smooth back and bundled him into our sack. He'd felt alien then. But now I could see him – this strange new life. I thought about fetching Mum's yellow rubber washing-up gloves, but Ned wouldn't have liked that.

'Come on,' my brother said.

I sighed, then took a step and another and another till I was beside them.

Leonard looked from Ned to me and back to Ned. His big fish eyes swivelled in his head.

'All right,' Ned said. 'Do it.'

Before I could think a moment more, I slid my arms around the merman's chest, under his arms. He was light, like I remembered. He wriggled and pushed away. He wasn't strong but his movements were quick and squirming.

'Right, right, right,' my brother said, taking hold of Leonard's arm.

My head began to swim. I swallowed, pushing down nausea.

Leonard let out a squeal, high-pitched and ghastly.

'OK, OK,' Ned whispered, turning the arm.

Another squeal.

Ned turned it again and again as Leonard squealed and writhed.

'OK, OK, OK.'

Then there was a wet sound, a slurp and plop, like when Dad used the plunger to clear the kitchen sink. It was done.

Ned dropped the arm. I dropped Leonard and fell to my knees. The merman slid back into the water. He snarled at us. He tested his arm. He looked from Ned to me, to Ned. Then he smiled his wide fishy smile.

Ned smiled back. 'We did it,' my brother said. 'All fixed.'

I blew out a long stream of air, picked myself up and grinned at Ned. 'We did,' I said.

All fixed.

Ned looked down at Leonard and scratched his chin. 'We've just got to put the sling on him,' he said.

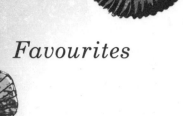

Favourites

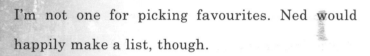

I'm not one for picking favourites. Ned would happily make a list, though.

Ned's favourite foods: macaroni cheese, frankfurters, scampi, Frazzles, apple crumble.

Ned's favourite places to go: the beach, the rock pools by Portland Bill. Dad's quarry on a Saturday with no one around. We'd put on hard hats and clamber and climb across the rocks and through tunnels. Ned always wanted to go further, stay longer. I guess it wasn't much of a day out for Dad, though.

Ned's favourite *Star Trek* episodes: this is a tough one. He had a list. It changed a lot. But always near the top was, 'The City on the Edge of Forever'. It's a good episode. It's got the best characters – Captain Kirk, Commander Spock and Doctor Leonard McCoy. It's got time travel. Kirk falls in love. All features of classic episodes.

The threesome travel through time to New York where Kirk falls in love with a lady called Edith. But because they change things in the past they no longer exist in the future. This makes sense in the programme, but when I've tried to explain it to Mum she says it sounds like nonsense.

The only way to make the future the way it should be is to let Edith die as she was meant to.

The episode's got one of Kirk's best lines, a favourite of Ned's. My brother likes to use it whenever it's time to go – *'Let's get the hell out of here.'*

Ned's favourite ways to spend an afternoon: exploring with me. Well, it used to be. We'd find some uncharted bit of Portland, a rocky bit of shore or the shrubland by an ancient church. Somewhere secret, and see what we could find, see what we could see.

But Leonard changed things. Even favourites.

Now Ned spent his afternoons in the garage. With or without me. Sometimes I'd find him gone, find him in the garage, sat on the edge of the tub, Leonard's head close to his. As I pushed open the door, his whispers and Leonard's clicks would stop.

I couldn't remember a time before when Ned didn't tell me everything. But now I got the feeling that it was Leonard who was hearing all of Ned's thoughts and worries and fears. Maybe that is how it worked. Maybe the child of Atargatis needed to listen, to hear it all before working a wonder. Maybe.

If this was the last big adventure, as Ned had said, it was *his* adventure, not ours. I looked on. I watched. I hoped. And sometimes jealousy clogged my throat.

Ned's other favourite way to spend an afternoon: worrying Mum. But this seemed to have stopped too. Mum had noticed as well.

Over lunch, one day, she asked what we were up to.

I looked to Ned.

He told her we were sorting out the salvage. 'A spring clean,' he said. 'And you said we couldn't go out.'

Mum narrowed her eyes. 'It's autumn and what I say doesn't usually stop you boys.'

'Mum,' Ned said, looking her in the eyes and reaching up to take her shoulder. 'We've turned over a new leaf. We will be the good boys you always longed for.' He spoilt his serious tone by cackling.

'Rubbish,' Mum said. 'You're up to something.'

I found myself wondering the same. What was Ned up to? What was Leonard up to? What was the plan?

Because all the time that Ned spent with Leonard, our little fishy friend, his arm in the wet sling was getting better. But my brother was not.

'It's nearly time,' Ned told me in the late afternoon as the autumn chill spread under the closed door of the garage and up our legs. He bent over in a coughing fit.

'Nearly time?' I asked. 'For what?'

Ned straightened, looked at me and tipped his head to one side. 'Nearly time to say goodbye,' he said, and turned towards Leonard, who was sat below the water.

I asked another question. 'We're letting him go?'

This one Ned did not answer.

If a miracle was coming, time was running short. Hope was slipping away.

My favourite thing to do: worry about Ned.

Plan

Dad likes big events. Like trips to London. He's not really there in the everyday. He goes to work early and when he gets home, filthy, he has a bath, we eat dinner, he sets us some maths to do, then he usually falls asleep in front of the TV, like Ned.

Sometimes, at the weekends, Dad has an 'event' planned. After he's watched his fill of *Grandstand* he'll say, 'Right, boys, we're going out.' And we go to the cinema or swimming pool or into town.

'What about the quarry today?' he said this weekend.

Mum coughed. 'Ned's been quite tired this week, Charlie. I think that's too much for him.'

'He can't just stay in for ever. We'll take it easy.'

'You can take it easy doing something else. Not the quarry.'

Dad pulled a face. The kind of face Ned pulled when he didn't get his way. 'Fine,' he said. 'Any bright ideas, boys?'

We were sat together in the front room. I'd been reading. Dad and Ned were watching *Grandstand*. Mum was humming and flicking through a magazine.

Bright ideas; I had none. Ned did, though.

'I was thinking about E.T., Dad.'

'Right . . .'

'The Extra-Terrestrial,' Ned continued. 'You know in the film when Elliott is escaping with E.T. and he's got that box on the front of his bike?'

Mum looked up from her magazine. 'And they fly to the moon?' she said.

Ned laughed.

I grinned. 'They don't fly to the moon, Mum.'

'I did think it was a bit far-fetched.'

'What about the box?' Dad asked.

Here it was. Ned's plan. Maybe this was what he and Leonard spent those afternoons whispering about. 'Can we make one to put on my bike?'

Dad smiled. 'That's a great idea. Easy. We can definitely do that.'

'Percussion first, though,' Mum said.

'Right. We'll go in half an hour. All right, boys?' Dad flicked the TV back on. Des Lynam, the *Grandstand* presenter with the thick moustache was interviewing Allan Wells, one of Dad's favourite athletes. Des was asking Allan whether he thought the Russians would come to the Olympics in Los Angeles next year.

'Good question, Des,' Dad said at the TV.

'Lie down, Ned,' Mum said. 'I'll get some tissue.'

Ned mouthed at me as I left. He seemed to be saying, *'Feet lemon.'*

I frowned at him.

My brother widened his eyes, bared his teeth and mimed eating.

'Oh. Feed Leonard,' I mouthed in reply.

'Half an hour,' Dad shouted as I snuck into the basement.

Usually, when Leonard saw Ned he smiled, all sharp teeth and glinting eyes. He never smiled at me though, and I didn't smile at him. He stared. I stared.

'I've brought fish,' I said, and waved the small pollock from the door.

Leonard didn't move. I threw the fish from

where I stood into the tub. Leonard clicked and gurgled.

'Why are you here, Leonard?' I asked.

Leonard clicked and snatched up the fish.

'Are you just lost, like E.T.?'

The merman took a bite, watching me.

'Do you have powers like him too? Are you here for Ned? Are you gonna do it? Make him better?'

Leonard gurgled again before slipping into the water where he sat below the surface and stared at me.

Mostly, in *Star Trek*, if the alien is good you can see it. They make it obvious, with bright lights and white clothes. As Leonard sat there, in the dark, with his finned head and sharp teeth, I wondered if I was hearing the stories wrong; how could Leonard be good while looking like that?

Leonard just stared and I realised that I did not know what this creature was. I wanted a miracle but I didn't know what kind of miracle Leonard would deliver. I wanted him gone.

For a moment, jealousy rose up and drowned all other thoughts, drowned out any hope of why the fish-man had come. I wanted my brother back and the creature that sat before me gone.

I swallowed down that feeling.

'Maybe you just want to go home, hey?' I opened the door. I could hear Ned's choking, spluttering. 'We'll send you home soon. Ned's got a plan. I think.'

The van made a racket. Dad always said he needed to get the fan belt looked at, but he never did. We screeched away from home.

The van was loud but Ned was louder. He

coughed and choked all the way into Weymouth. All the way to the hardware shop.

Every time we tried to talk, my brother would open his mouth but all that came out was that wet rattle. In the end we fell silent. We listened to the engine scream and Ned choke.

As we parked by James & Sons, I wondered how much hope Dad had. Did he have anything better to rely on than a little green man?

We got wood, a big sheet of it. Some strips of metal. Bolts – Dad spent about ten minutes discussing the right size with the man in the shop. A new drill bit to go through the metal. Some L-shaped brackets – 'They'll go inside the box. Make sure it's good and solid,' Dad said.

Ned fell asleep on the way back. Dad carried him inside and laid him on the sofa. Mum had lunch waiting for us.

'Just me and you then, Jamie,' Dad said, placing his ham and piccalilli sandwich back down on the plate, unbitten.

Dad's good with his hands. At Christmas, Mum makes the cake and then Dad makes little models of snowmen or robins to go on top of it. Dad fixes everything at home – the washing machine, cabinets, the plumbing. He always shows Ned and I what to do. We're allowed in his cupboard under the stairs, where hammers and saws hang on hooks and a little set of drawers holds all sorts of nails and screws and washers and bits and bobs. We're not allowed to touch the power tools, though.

Dad pushed the white and pink and yellow sandwich away. 'Might let you do a little drilling today.'

It was a little thing but it made me smile.

We fetched the tools from the cupboard under the stairs and started on Ned's bike. We measured up how big the box should be. We sawed the wood into sections.

'Keep the saw straight,' Dad said. 'Otherwise the teeth'll catch.'

I wanted to tell Dad about Leonard. I wanted to ask him if he believed in miracles or magic, if he believed in the impossible. Dad's never been much of a talker though, and I'd promised Ned.

Instead, we drilled, and I got to do a little as promised. Then we screwed the wood together, using the L-shaped brackets.

'Give it a wiggle then,' Dad said.

I gave it a wiggle. It was good and solid.

I nearly asked about the hospital, about the doctors, about Ned's chances. I nearly asked but I didn't.

Finally we fixed the box to the bike. The bolts weren't the right size for the ready-made holes

in the frame. Dad shook his head and said the man in the shop didn't know what he was talking about. He carefully made the holes larger with his new drill bit. He made more holes in the strips of metal and more still in our box. Then we bolted it in place.

'There we go,' Dad said, giving the whole thing a shake. 'You could have someone sit in there.'

'Good,' I said. After all, that was the plan.

'Shall we call it a day there?' Dad said.

I wanted to say no. I wanted to sit him down and make him tell me how it was all going to be OK. I wanted him to tell me how he was planning to make everything better.

But he didn't have a plan. No one had a plan.

Except for Ned.

We called it a day but Ned still slept. Mum said I should go and see Lucy. We always used to knock for Lucy. I said I didn't fancy it. Mum insisted.

I knocked quietly, hoping no one would hear. But the door opened instantly. Little Pete stood there, as if he'd been waiting for someone.

'Hello,' he shouted.

'Hi,' I said.

Mrs Taylor appeared. 'Hi, Jamie. It's lovely to see you. Lucy will be delighted.'

She was. She was delighted to show me the artwork she'd been doing at school, delighted to tell me about the dance competition coming up, delighted to gossip about other kids at school.

I couldn't share her delight, and eventually her chatter grew slower and I stopped filling any gaps.

'Cluedo!' she said. And we played. Colonel Mustard did it, in the library with the lead pipe.

After the game, when I was still silent and staring, Lucy said, 'Are you OK, Jamie?'

I stared a moment then shook my head. 'Not really.'

Peewee appeared then, dressed as a robot. 'I am pa robop,' he chanted in a machine voice.

I smiled a moment. Then said, 'I've got to go.'

Later, when he woke, I tried to talk to Ned about the plan. 'What's Leonard here for?' I asked.

My brother, still lying on the sofa, didn't answer. Eventually he said, 'Isn't it obvious, Jamie?'

But I shook my head. 'He's gonna make you better?' Hope was in my words but it was fast escaping from my heart.

Ned shook his head again and coughed. 'Jamie,

I'm really sick. The new medicine isn't working.'

I couldn't speak; we didn't talk about the illness. I stared at him, so quick with a smile, with a laugh.

Ned closed his eyes. A single tear squeezed through and ran down onto the cushion. 'Our last adventure,' he whispered before falling back to sleep.

Sorrow

Grandad spread out a map on the table. Ned and I shifted our glasses of squash.

'Right. Britain,' Grandad said. 'Where are we?'

Portland was in front of Ned, at the far south. I had the west. Grandad the east. Ned's finger squashed our island.

'Yep,' Grandad nodded. 'You can point to where it is. Now *tell* me where it is.'

Even though Grandad mostly told us stories, it seemed to me that he was a good teacher.

'It's on the south coast,' I said.

'It's near Weymouth,' Ned said.

'It's between Southampton and Exeter.'

'It's in Dorset.'

Grandad nodded. 'OK. Let's go west,' he said.

Ned traced the curve of Chesil Beach round to West Bay then west through coastal towns we knew and on to Exeter.

'Exeter,' Grandad said, 'is in Devon. That's the next county west.'

Ned's finger followed the coast south through Torquay and Dartmouth and round, west again to Plymouth.

'There it is,' Grandad said.

Plymouth was home to Grandad once upon a time. It was where Dad was born when Grandad was away at sea. It was where Grandma was buried before Ned and I were born.

'What's that river there?' Grandad pointed to the west of Plymouth.

I was closest and squinted at the tiny text. 'The Tamar,' I said.

'T-A-M-A-R. Pronounced *Tay-mar*,' Grandad said.

We nodded. I mouthed, 'Tay-mar.'

'That's it. That's a border, between Devon and Cornwall, the furthest county west. Keep going.'

I took over from Ned and ran my finger across the shiny map. The towns had strange names now. Almost foreign. Polperro. Mevagissey. Landewednack. Cornwall kept going, west and west and west till we hit Land's End.

'That is the very furthest west you can go,' Grandad said, 'before you have to take to the sea. The place we are looking for is a little further round. Can you find Zennor, Jamie?'

We continued our journey, heading round the coast and back east. Zennor was not far. A tiny village. A dot on the map.

'Here we are then,' Grandad said. 'I've got

another mermaid story for you. Happened right there, in Zennor. Do you remember Gin?'

We'd never met him, but we remembered Gin. He was first mate on Grandad's first captaincy after leaving Long Ben in Manila, a fishing boat out of Plymouth.

'*Well, he had a story for me once. Said it was about his great, great, great-grandfather's brother or some such. A man by the name of Mathew Trewella.*

'*You wouldn't have heard of him, Gin said. But in Zennor and round abouts, his was a famous name. Even more famous in his day. It's said that Mathew had the most beautiful voice imaginable. He sang wherever he went, through the village and about his work as a carpenter, always singing. Every Sunday he sung in the church in Zennor. Everyone* stopped when he sang.

'But they say that his voice changed. Over the course of a year, his joyful singing became a sad dirge. Still beautiful. But now, instead of bringing a smile, it brought tears.

'They started saying, in Zennor, that Mathew was bedevilled. They whispered that he'd been seen on the cliffs around the village with a mysterious lady in black. They muttered about witchcraft and wondered whether it was right to have the man sing in their church.

'Mathew had a brother – Gin's great, great, great-grandfather, older than Mathew, living in another village. When this older brother heard these whispers, he returned to Zennor and found the singer on the quayside, singing to the sea. He barely recognised Mathew's pale face, so ghostly.

'Mathew laughed at the idea of sorcery, his cheeks forming deep hollows. "I'm not bewitched," he told his brother. "I'm sick."

'Mathew took his brother back to his home where his carpentry tools sat unused and the unwashed smell of sickness filled the air. The older brother aired the house, cleaned and cooked a clear fish soup.

'As the two brothers went to sleep, Mathew on his bed, the older brother below the table, the singer whispered, "Don't worry, brother. I think I've found a way to be well again."

'The next day was a church day. Mathew stood and sang a song that no one in Zennor had heard before. Or perhaps they'd heard it all their

lives, cos in that song was the wash of
the sea, the roar of the wind and the
gulls' call. Mathew sang up a storm in
that tiny church. And when the last
note fell, no one moved, apart from
Mathew. He walked down the aisle to
a lady who had slipped into the
back row as the young man sang,
a tiny lady dressed all in black.

'Mathew walked out of that building, following
that mysterious woman, who left the church with
three long, floating bounds. He was never seen
again. All his brother found was the woman's
black shawl, discarded on the rocky shore.

'They say in Zennor that you can hear Mathew
still. On a calm night, when the sky is clear, his
sweet voice rings over the village, filled with pure
joy again. They whisper, in Zennor, of mermaids

living beneath the waves, watching the town. They mutter, when men go away to sea, of the foolish dream, of seeking Mathew's maid.'

Ned nodded as the story ended.

I frowned. 'The mermaid took him?'

'Well, Gin called the story "Mathew's Choice",' Grandad said. 'I think he went with the mermaid willingly. I think he went to live a . . . different kind of life.'

Ned still nodded. My brother's face spoke of understanding.

I frowned.

Still I told my heart that Leonard was there to fix my brother. I told my heart that was the story we were in.

My heart told me I lied. My heart felt an ending coming that no one could control.

Melody

The sky was clear the night we let Leonard out for fresh air, for a taste of the outside, to prepare to send him home. A cool, clear night. Dad was asleep on the sofa. Mum was in the bath.

We needed to be quiet; Ned was meant to be warm and safe inside, but was coming out for fresh air and a taste of the outside too.

When we peered into the garage, Leonard's eyes were vast. They glowed in the gloom. A soft light.

'Come on, Len,' Ned said from the door. 'Come outside. Move out the way, Jamie.'

I stepped back out of the garage and retreated to the garden fence, bordering the cliff. The cliff that fell down, down to the sea, the Channel. The moon shone and rippled across the calm sea. In the quiet, in the night, you could hear the waves crashing on the rocks below.

'Come on,' Ned whispered again to the merman.

It was dark. Just the moon's beams and the light that escaped the bathroom window above showed Leonard peering from the back door. He smiled and breathed in deep.

'This is our garden,' Ned said.

With that Leonard sprang. Three leaps and he was beside me, perched on the fence. He no longer wore the makeshift sling.

Ned barked a laugh and a cough.

Leonard clicked and gurgled and gazed down at the sea below.

'Home,' I whispered, nodding.

Ned wheezed up beside us. 'Did you see that? Amazing. If I could move like that . . . You're amazing, Leonard.'

I stared at my brother as he stared at the fish-man, who stared out at the sea.

My brother's words rang in my ears – *our last adventure*. I wanted it over. Hope was gone and something like fear was creeping in.

'We've got to let him go home, Ned,' I whispered. 'We can't keep him.'

My brother looked up at me. 'Not yet, Jamie. It's not time. Not yet.'

'Soon,' I whispered.

'Soon.'

As we stood in the cool night, Leonard began to sing. Quietly at first. The notes collided with the sounds of the waves below, and like the sky and sea on a clear day, it was hard to know where one began and the other ended. We stood and listened a long time. Leonard smiled and sang. Ned smiled and hummed. My brother's tune joined with the merman's and joined with the lapping sea. If the song had not filled my mind, I would have thought of another song, on a boat, in a beautiful cove: Perla's parting song.

I was on the outside of that sound, looking in, as the song went on and on into the distance and into the future. Leonard sang and Ned opened his mouth and sang. It was not two songs but one song with two singers. There was no part in it for me. For a moment that fear became a thought – *I was losing my brother*. A tear rolled down my cheek and fell.

Suddenly a voice broke the night air and the song stopped. 'What you got there, boys?'

I whipped round. Ned stepped in front of

Leonard. We expected to see Mum in her dressing gown, calling from the back door. The light was still on in the bathroom. But from over the fence next door, one point of orange glowed – Mrs Clarke's cigarette.

'Is that a cat?' our neighbour croaked.

'Yeah,' my brother called back. 'It's . . . er . . . a cat, Mrs Clarke.'

'That ain't no cat.'

'Erm . . .' I said, and glanced over my shoulder at Leonard.

'It is. It's one of them . . . what is it called, Jamie . . . ? Hairless cats, Mrs Clarke.'

'Siamese cat,' I called.

The glowing cigarette waved in the air. Our neighbour's mutters were lost in the gap between us. As my eyes adjusted, I began to see the roses, the reds and pinks, turned black and purple in the night, and the old lady, leaning over our fence.

'Bring it here then,' Mrs Clarke called.

I glanced up at the bathroom window, where Mum was not to be disturbed.

'Let's see *this cat*,' she shouted.

I searched for an excuse.

Ned spoke first. 'It's gone. It ran off when you yelled.'

I glanced back again and could see Ned wasn't lying; Leonard was gone.

The bathroom light switched off as Mrs Clarke went back to her muttering. The back door swung open.

'Ned, what are you doing out here?' Mum called to us, then she saw our neighbour. 'Oh, sorry, Mrs Clarke,' she said.

'Have you got a cat?' the old lady asked.

'A cat?'

'Ned says you've got a Siamese cat.'

Ned coughed. All eyes were on him. The cough became a fit. Mum hurried over. Her dressing gown held tight as it tried to stream out behind her.

'Not our cat,' Ned spluttered. His foot flicked out and kicked my shin.

'No . . . erm . . . it was just here. It's gone.'

'They were singing with it,' Mrs Clarke called.

Mum stroked Ned's back. She looked at me. Her eyes narrowed. 'Get inside, boys. I'll talk to the old . . . our dear neighbour,' she whispered just for us.

'It didn't look much like a cat,' Mrs Clarke said.

Mum's lips were thin, her eyebrow drawn. 'Inside.'

Ned coughed all the way in. He coughed as

we sat at the table and waited. He coughed as I whispered to him that Mum would find Leonard. He shook his head as he coughed.

'What do you think you were doing?' Mum asked, still angry, when she returned from the garden.

She hadn't found him. If she had, she'd be asking about the merman. Ned still coughed. It was left to me to lie.

'It was just a cat.'

'I don't care about the cat. Why, why would you be outside? In the cold. In the dark.' Mum stroked Ned's back. His coughing stopped as he spat into a handkerchief that Mum held out.

Later, in our bedroom, after Mum had stopped shouting and crying and telling me I had to look after my brother, Ned was by the window, staring.

I knew why he sat so silent. He was listening for Leonard's song, for their song.

We sat in silence but for the sound of the waves and the gentle grunt of Dad's snoring downstairs. The television went on. The nine o'clock news. Somewhere on the street a door closed.

'I'm going to find him,' Ned said.

'What?'

'I'm going out.' Ned pulled his jumper tight. 'Pass me my coat.'

'You heard what Mum said,' I hissed.

Ned left the window and fetched his coat himself. He zipped it to the top. 'You coming?'

'I . . .' I said. 'Hang on. Listen.'

We stopped again, still and silent. And there it was. Mixed with the sound of crashing waves. Leonard's song. Ned sighed. It sounded like our friend had found his way back to the garage.

My face became all frown. 'We've got to send him home, Ned,' I said.

'It's not time yet. I'm going to check he's OK.'

'You can't!' I whispered. 'If you're going, you're going alone.' I sat on the edge of the bed.

Ned stared at me and, nodded once. 'OK,' he said. 'I'll go alone.'

Fomalhaut

Mum's always been a worrier. Dad says we shouldn't give her more reason to worry. I try to follow this instruction. Ned does not.

As I sat listening for my brother's return, I realised I took after Mum in the worry department. I should have gone with him. He should not have been out in the cold, in the dark with Leonard – Leonard, that strange creature who could do, would do, *might* do strange things.

But Ned returned. Leonard was safe and sound in his tub.

'We've got to let him go,' I said again.

I got the same reply. 'Soon.'

The next day, Mum's worry was at new heights. She took Ned's temperature every few hours and his percussion was extra vigorous. She spent a whole episode of *Star Trek* on the phone to the doctors.

Ned had put on 'Arena', the first episode that sees Kirk in a fist fight on a strange planet. We both agreed, as the captain fought the Gorn, that the alien looked a little like Leonard. The big eyes. The fins across his head. The sharp-toothed mouth. One big difference – the Gorn was made of rubber.

'The doctor says you must stay wrapped up warm,' Mum said after she'd put down the phone and Kirk had spared the alien's life.

'It took an hour for the doctor to say that,' Ned said.

'Please, Ned.' There were almost tears in Mum's voice.

Ned stayed warm. I went out to feed Leonard. I stared at him. He was still a stranger to me. He stared right back.

'You've got to go,' I said to him as I threw a fillet of plaice into the tub. 'Go and leave my brother alone. He's not got enough time, not for *you and me*. Go!'

The day crept by. Mum's worry washed in and out. Dad returned home to find her in tears. He called Grandad and took Mum out for dinner in Weymouth. She left strict instructions: 'They are not to leave this house.' We sat with Grandad in the kitchen.

'Do you remember the Southern Fish?' he asked me.

'*Piscis Austrinus,*' Ned said.

'What is this?' Grandad laughed. 'I must really

149

have you with these mermaid stories if you're telling them to each other now.'

Ned nodded. 'You do, Grandad.'

'OK. Do you remember which star of *Piscis Austrinus* you can see?'

Ned didn't remember; maybe I hadn't told him that part.

I did. 'Fomalhaut.'

'Ah ha,' Grandad said. 'Fomalhaut. *Fum al-hut*. The fish's mouth. It's arrived.'

'What?'

Ned's question brought on a mini-lesson on how the Earth moves round the sun. Through the summer, we're on one side of our own star. We see all the stars that stare back at our sun from that side. By the winter, we're on the other side of the sun. Our night sky has completely changed to show a new set of stars, shining down.

'Fomalhaut appears, low in the sky, in the autumn. It's arrived.'

I thought about that *soon*. I wondered what Ned was waiting for, what Leonard was waiting for. Could this be it?

Ned leaped up from the table. 'Let's go and see.'

'No, no. We are not leaving the house,' Grandad said. 'Breaking your mother's command would be more than my life is worth. Let's see, though. Erm . . .' Grandad started looking around, pointing. 'Where are we?' he muttered. Then he got up. 'Right, living-room window.'

We crowded by the small window.

'Get the light, Jamie,' Grandad said, pulling the window open. The sound of the sea flooded in. The curtains flapped. 'This is south,' he said as I turned the lights off. 'Look there.' He pointed to a big blank space, black and black and black.

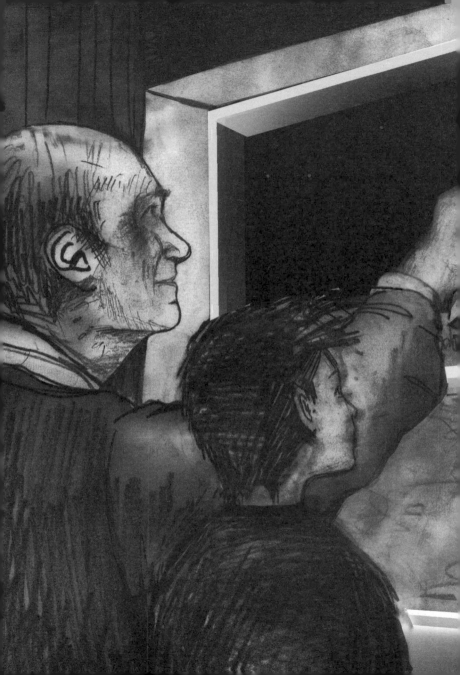

And there it was. The only star in all that black.

'They call it the loneliest star,' Grandad said.

'Good name,' Ned said.

I nodded and stared and thought about Ned and Leonard's lonely song. I thought about *going alone*. I thought about saying goodbye before we were ready. I thought about loneliness. It stretched out before me.

Time

Ned's got a ton of clothes that don't fit him. Gran insists on sending clothes every birthday and every Christmas. No matter how often Mum tells her our sizes, she buys them to fit our age. Mine are a little too small, and Ned's are a mile too big.

Before she let us out, Mum stuffed Ned in an assortment of jumpers. She started with ones that fitted him right up to my biggest one.

'Is four jumpers a bit much, Mum?' Ned said.

'Two of them are very thin. The doctor said, keep warm.'

Ned threw me a look that said Mum had lost the plot. His eyes were wide, the bottom of his mouth slanted to one side.

I grinned but held onto my laugh. I was beginning to think that Mum's worries were not as mad as Ned made out. I was beginning to feel time shrink.

'Don't let him take them off, Jamie,' Mum said. 'I'm just going to the shops. I'll be half an hour tops. Do not leave the garden.'

'Right, let's get the hell out of here,' Ned said.

Mum sighed.

In the garage, Ned quickly pulled off two jumpers.

Leonard stared. Leonard wore no clothes.

'You must have a mum, Len,' Ned said, dumping the clothes by the door. 'Are all mums mad?'

'She's just trying to look after you, Ned.' I handed him the bag of frozen sprats.

'Do you honestly think that two jumpers

will make a difference? That any of it will help?' he whispered.

I had nothing to say to this. As my brother turned to the merman, a tear swam in my eye.

Leonard crunched through the raw fish.

No one spoke. Ned coughed a little. Leonard shook his head and put a hand to my brother's chest.

I wiped my tear away. Leonard had promised so much with a touch and a look. I'd thought he knew. I'd thought he brought hope.

'Nothing will help,' my brother whispered, quieter still.

Phrases ran through my mind: 'It will all be OK,' and 'Keep your chin up.' They ran through my mind and out the other side.

Nothing will help, I said to myself.

Silence again for long minutes until a ring and a knock. Someone at the front door.

'Anyone home?' called a deep voice.

'Mr Taylor?' my brother said.

'Officer Taylor,' I said.

We knew Anthony Taylor well. He lived on our road. He was Lucy and Peewee's dad.

But there were two Anthony Taylors.

Mr Taylor went to the pub with Dad. Dad called him Tone. He loved his car and spent Sunday mornings washing it. He won the parents' race at last year's sports day.

Officer Taylor was a serious man. He frowned from under his policeman's hat. He'd brought Ned home twice, when he'd disappeared on one of those days he'd wanted to escape.

It was Officer Taylor we saw standing at our front door, when we appeared from round the side of the garage.

'Hello, lads,' he said.

'Hello, Mr Taylor,' I said.

'All right, Tone,' Ned said.

'Is your mum home?'

I shook my head.

'She's abandoned us, Officer.' Ned grinned.

'Not to worry. You can probably help. It's not something we'd usually follow up, but given as she's a . . . neighbour . . . Mrs Clarke reported a strange sighting in your garage or in your garden.'

My mouth opened.

Ned nodded.

'I told her I'd check it out. And you know' – he dropped to a whisper and glanced at the house next door – 'she's always watching.' Back to his normal voice. 'So I'm just stopping by. Can I have a quick glance around your garage?'

'Erm,' I said.

'It was a cat,' Ned said.

'Just a quick look, boys.'

'Well,' Ned said. 'Maybe we should wait till my mum gets home.'

'Come on, I'll just be a minute.'

The door squeaked open. The light was off. The bulb was still broken. There was a small splash and a pat-pat sound.

I saw him move. I'm sure Ned saw him too. I don't know what the policeman saw as he peered into the gloom.

'What was that?' he said.

I shook my head.

'There's been this cat,' Ned said. 'Keeps sleeping in our garage.'

I turned my shake to a nod.

Officer Taylor pulled the door open a little more and stepped into the garage. He flicked on the light switch and looked up at the broken bulb when nothing happened.

'You're not messing around here, are you, lads?' he said.

'What?' my brother replied.

'You know it's an offence to disturb most wildlife, don't you?' Mr Taylor stepped into the garage. He pulled a torch from his belt and shone it towards the tub. The surface rippled. Leonard was gone. The policeman shone his torch under the bath and round at the shelves. The light stopped on a box high on a shelf. A cow's skull lay beside it, not on top. The policeman walked towards it.

'Oop! There it goes,' Ned said, spinning on the spot.

'What?' The torch was on us.

'The cat,' Ned said. 'Just ran out.'

Mr Taylor looked at me.

'It was quick,' I said.

Outside, in the light again, the policeman wrote a few words in his notebook. 'Thanks, lads,' he said. 'Hopefully that keeps our *neighbour* happy.'

We nodded and waved goodbye.

I shook and sighed when Mr Taylor had disappeared down the road. 'It's time,' I said. 'We've got to let him go. We can't carry on like this.'

Ned sighed. He looked at his feet. 'I thought I'd know when it was time. I thought I'd be ready.'

'What?'

My brother shook his head and coughed. He looked up at me and nodded. 'You're right. It's time.'

Pause

We'd agreed it was time so we made plans. We'd take Leonard back to the sea and we'd do it at night. It must be at night. We had Ned's E.T. box on the front of his bike to put him in. There was the spot, halfway down to the beach, where the path split, and at the end of the left branch the rocks made stepping stones out to a platform that stuck into the sea, like a tongue tasting the salty waves. That's where we'd send him home.

But still we waited. Ned could not just let him go. Maybe he was still waiting to be ready. That first night, after the policeman had come knocking, my brother asked for 'a little more time'.

The next day was spent with Grandad, looking at maps and playing Risk. Grandad won. Ned sat glumly while Grandad's red troops decimated his yellows. I couldn't think straight. I couldn't remember the first three presidents of the United States – *George Washington, John Adams, Thomas Jefferson*. I couldn't tell Grandad which river passed through Istanbul – *the Bosphorus*. The names of the twins who are said to have founded Rome were lost to me – *Romulus and Remus*.

'What's wrong with you boys today?' Grandad asked.

We both shrugged.

'Well, my mermaid stories are all run out. So I can't help there. Hmm. Shall we get chips for lunch?'

'All right,' Ned said; chips are always a winner.

★

I was ready to do it that night. I'd fed Leonard and told him that it was time to go home. I'd found our warmest clothes and pushed them under the bed, ready. But Ned's cough was worse than ever. He lay on the sofa, choking.

Water streamed from his eyes as Mum rubbed his chest. Dad looked angry as he watched. I sat by the living-room window and stared out at Fomalhaut, the lonely star.

Later, as Mum fixed Ned a drink – Dad had fallen asleep – I said I'd do it, I'd take him.

Ned sat up and spluttered through his cough, 'You can't, Jamie. He can't go without me. Surely you understand that.'

I frowned at my brother.

He shook his head, coughed and lay back down.

Ned was still coughing downstairs when I was sent to bed.

*

He slept long into the next morning. I woke before him.

Mum made me write about the fox book. The boy, Billy, had to let the fox cub go. It was sad. But you could see that life would still work. I thought I should tell Ned about it; we didn't need Leonard. Life worked without him.

Mum sat beside me and stared and sighed. Her eyes were red.

When Ned woke, he was still exhausted. He brought his duvet downstairs and watched *Star Trek*.

Mum brought us macaroni cheese with frankfurters in it.

'My favourite,' Ned said.

As 'The City on the Edge of Forever' ended and Kirk said his parting line, Ned turned to me. 'Tonight,' he said. He'd only managed a few mouthfuls of his pasta.

'You sure?'

My brother glared at me. His eyes were dark. 'Tonight,' he said. 'I'm ready. It's time.'

Chase

We stayed up late, whispering. Ned asked me to tell him all of the mermaid stories again. The Japanese captain. Atargatis. The mermaid of Zennor. Long Ben and Perla.

We listened to the stairs creak as Mum and Dad climbed. We waited for another hour after their bedroom door shut. And it was in that hour that my eyes closed and I drifted into sleep.

I was awoken by a peal of thunder. Ned was gone. Alone.

I leaped up, still dressed, and bounded silently down the stairs.

Outside, there was little light. Cloud covered the moon. I looked for Fomalhaut but could not find it.

The front gate clanked shut. I could hear Ned already pedalling away.

'Ned!'

Thunder called again, drowning my shout. I ran for my bike. A drop of rain hit my nose as I flung the front gate open. It quickly became a drizzle.

The street was quiet. There were no lights on. I squinted ahead.

Ned was there, not taking the path behind our house, which wound round and round and down and down. He stayed on the road – it dropped down to join the path someway along.

I pedalled quickly, calling to him, hearing only his cough in reply. The rain fell heavier but I was catching up.

I saw the car before I heard it. The headlights hit Ned, then me. I watched Ned swerve to the left. Officer Taylor peered into the night at my brother, then me.

Ned swore loudly.

'Ned!' I shouted.

'Lads,' the policeman called, but we were gone, flying downhill.

I left the road and joined the path as the headlights lit upon me again.

'Ned! Jamie!' Officer Taylor shouted.

I could not see my brother. I could still hear his hacking cough, though. The path was slick. Mud spat up as my wheels slithered beneath me. I glanced back.

'Come on, boys. You'll break your necks,' I heard on the wind. I didn't stop.

I pictured Leonard's huge eyes squinting ahead. As the rain fell heavier still, I pedalled harder and missed the spot I was looking for.

My brakes screeched and my wheels lost all grip. I flew forward and got a faceful of mud and grit, my arm twisting painfully beneath me.

Ned's bike lay discarded. The moon shone off the sea and I could see Ned again – he was disappearing over the rocks with the merman following.

I picked myself up and ran. A torch's beam jumped up and down as Mr Taylor chased us.

'Jamie!' he shouted again. 'Ned!'

I leaped from wet rock to wet rock. I lost my footing a few times, finally crashing down on the stone.

Leonard was almost home, he and Ned bounding ahead. My brother's jumps almost matched the merman's. He was not the sick boy who lay choking. Tonight he was transformed. There was life I had not seen in a long time. He was reborn.

I lay breathless and bruised, watching.

Leonard and Ned, Ned and Leonard crouched together where the rocks ended. Some whispered words, some quiet clicks passing between them.

'LADS!' the policeman roared; he'd reached the bikes.

Ned leaned forward and whispered once more in Leonard's ear. My heart roared with jealousy. *Our adventure*, Ned had said.

I pushed myself upwards and strained to reach my brother.

The merman's huge eyes swivelled as he sat there perched on the edge. He smiled at me, then suddenly he leaped through the rain and into the waiting waves that swirled below.

He bobbed for a moment, then looked up at Ned.

I watched as Ned reached into his pocket. The

moon lit upon the carved bone whale as he leaned down towards the merman's outstretched hand.

Suddenly Mr Taylor's torch beam shone round and round like a lighthouse. I looked back.

'LADS!' he called again.

There was a splash. I turned quickly but Ned was gone. The waves still swirled but no heads bobbed above them.

I wanted to dive, to save my brother, but without him all courage was lost, all boldness gone.

'HELP!' I screamed. 'HELP!'

An age came and went before the policeman barrelled past me, flicking off his shoes and leaping into the cold sea.

Through the rain and my tears I couldn't see. My words flew away on the wind. 'Please help.'

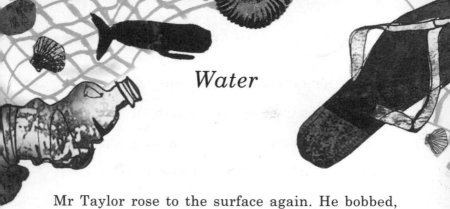

Water

Mr Taylor rose to the surface again. He bobbed, looking down.

The waves sprayed up and the rain fell down. My eyes filled with tears.

The policeman dived down again.

Now my body began to shake. It was the cold or the shock or the sobs that rocked through me.

Then the waves broke. Tony's dark hair. His eyes were searching, not down but up now, at me, at the ledge. There was another head and the policeman was holding a frail body.

'Ned!' I screamed.

Tony grunted as he pushed Ned up and out, onto the rock. He pulled himself out, grabbed my brother and pulled Ned's body up to his ear.

'No, no, no,' Mr Taylor hissed. He threaded his fingers together and laid them across Ned's wet chest. The fingers flexed and pushed down as hard as Mum's percussion.

I was glued to the stone. A statue.

Mr Taylor grabbed Ned's nose and brought his lips down to my brother's. Ned's chest rose and fell as the policeman blew.

Then he writhed and Mr Taylor knelt up. Water shot out of Ned's mouth like a volcano — water and vomit. Mr Taylor rolled him on his side.

He stared upwards and whispered a string of swear words and thanks.

I sprang forwards and grabbed Ned. Over his shoulder, through my tears, I saw Fomalhaut, winking down at me.

'Ned,' I cried.

My brother coughed and whispered, 'He's gone.'

I ignored him and squeezed harder.

In 'The Tholian Web', the crew of the *Enterprise* believe they've lost Captain Kirk. They even hold a funeral for him. Spock and Doctor McCoy play a recording that Kirk made in case he ever left them – his final message, asking them to work together, not argue. They go forward without him.

I thought about the day that Ned would leave. The day we knew was coming. Would I be able to go forward without him? Would all boldness leave? What would I be without Ned, without Captain Kirk?

At the end of the episode, they get Kirk back, rescue him from the sub-space rift. The captain is disappointed when McCoy tells him they hadn't yet heard his final message, but surprised to hear how well he and Spock had worked together.

What would Ned's final message be? Would he leave one?

Hospital

The rain had almost stopped as we ran and stumbled back up, towards home. I'd brought Ned's bike and left mine discarded where I'd crashed. Mr Taylor carried Ned and left his shoes by the rocks.

All the way, Ned complained that he could walk.

Mr Taylor kept saying things like, 'What the hell did you think you were doing?' and 'You're bleeding lucky I saw you.' And 'What will your parents say?' He didn't give Ned a chance to answer.

We found his car squashed against the hedge that lined the road. Mr Taylor threw Ned's bike in the boot and we got in the back. The car sped through the dark, sprays of mud flicking up from the screeching wheels.

We stopped outside our house. 'Let's get in,' Mr Taylor said. The policeman pounded on the front door before I could get my keys out.

A light went on upstairs and we heard Dad shout, 'What the hell . . . ?'

The stairs creaked as I pushed the door open.

'What's going on?' Dad said.

Mum cried as she stripped Ned's clothes off in front of everyone and threw towels around him.

'Tone doesn't want to see my wing-wah,' Ned complained.

Mum just cried and Dad grew angry as Mr Taylor told them what had happened. Ned and I filled in the blanks.

'I was just chasing him,' I said. 'I woke up and he'd gone.'

'I wanted to see the stars,' Ned lied. 'I wanted to see Fomalhaut.'

'You can see the stars from your bleeding window!' Dad shouted.

'Your grandfather and his stories!' Mum cried.

'I think Ned's all right—' Mr Taylor said.

Mum interrupted. 'We're going to the hospital.'

'Yeah, you'll want to get him checked out.'

'Now,' Mum said.

Dad thanked Tone and grabbed our coats. Mum still cried and asked Ned again and again, 'How could you? How *could* you?'

'Why didn't you wake us?' Dad asked me.

I just said, 'It was so quick; I didn't think.'

'He's a bit of a hero really,' the policeman said.

'I was following Jamie. I don't think I would have seen where Ned went without him.'

Dad grabbed me in a half-hug. I didn't feel like a hero.

Ned coughed and shivered and looked sicker than he ever had.

Mr Taylor left – he had to get up for Lucy's *dance thing* in the morning – still dripping, followed by hurried thank yous from Mum and Dad. Dad threw my coat at me and I put it over my wet clothes. Mum put hers over her nightie.

'He needs clothes,' Mum said.

Dad ran up the stairs and came back with layers and layers for Ned. 'Let's go.'

Ned dressed in the car. His cough grew worse and his shiver became a shake.

They knew us at the hospital. The nurse took

one look at Ned and fetched the doctor. We were whisked away down corridors, to a large room.

Doctors and nurses, Mum and Dad crowded round my brother. I sat on a hard chair in my damp clothes.

I don't remember falling asleep. I remember the cold and damp and dark. Then nothing. Then it was light and I was curled in a softer chair, wearing just my underwear with a rough hospital blanket around me.

Ned lay in a narrow bed. His chest rose and fell. Wires stretched from beneath his sheets to machines that flashed and bleeped. Mum knelt by the bed, her eyes red and wide. Dad was asleep on the hard chair.

'Mum,' I whispered. 'Ned?'

Her eyes did not move from Ned's quiet face. 'Grandad's coming to get you.'

He came, not long after. He and Dad whispered by the door.

'Come on, Jamie,' Grandad called, smiling at me.

I found my clothes, laid out on a radiator and dry now. I pulled them on and smelled the stormy sea.

I looked at Ned one more time, then Mum, then Dad. They both stared at my brother.

What would we be without him?

Grandad took me by the shoulder. 'Come on,' he said.

Words

I cried in the car all the way back, through Weymouth, along the road next to Chesil Beach, up to Grandad's bungalow. Grandad told me I wasn't to worry. He told me Ned was in good hands. But I knew what Ned had said – *nothing helps*. He was flotsam, helpless, bobbing on the vast sea.

All day, I cried and Grandad talked. Ned had pneumonia, he told me. He'd be in the hospital for a while. I cried and Grandad tried to make me eat. I managed a few chips. I cried and watched TV.

In the evening, Dad came. They whispered again. I was left out of another conversation.

Dad took me home. Mr Taylor had left Ned's bike out by the front door so I wheeled it round to the garage. The door stood open and I pushed the bike in and leaned it against a wall. I stood in the still and quiet and watched the calm water in Leonard's tub.

I thought about the moment I turned at Officer Taylor's call. Did Ned fall? Did he jump? Or had the creature that we'd sheltered pulled my brother in?

I kicked the tub and it filled the garage with a low ringing note. The water swirled.

After a time, some unknown length of time, Dad called me in again.

We talked in the kitchen, with bowls of tinned ravioli growing cold in front of us.

'I'm sorry, Dad,' I said.

Dad scratched his neck and frowned. 'Jamie,'

he said, 'you did your best. Right?'

I swallowed on nothing and stirred the orange sauce with my fork.

'You heard Tony. He wouldn't have found Ned without you.'

I lifted the fork and stared at the pasta speared on the prongs.

'It's not your fault.'

It wasn't? Maybe if I'd not kept Ned's secret, if I'd shown that little merman to Grandad on that first day or to Mum or Dad, or if I'd told the policeman even, when he came looking . . . ? Maybe Ned would not have gone alone. Maybe I'd have been there to hold him back. But then again, no one could stop Ned when he had a plan.

'What's gonna happen?' I said.

'The doctor . . .' Dad began. 'The doctor says he hopes . . . He's gonna be OK.'

*

The next morning, when we went in to see him, Ned didn't seem OK. Wires and tubes still connected him to bleeping machines.

Dad had brought clean clothes for Mum. He pulled her away from the bed and took her to shower and change. She gave me a brief flicker of a smile as they left me with Ned.

I thought he was asleep, but as soon as the door closed his eyes cracked open.

'Jamie,' he said with a thin grin.

'Ned.'

'You should have been down there. It was amazing.'

'What?'

The door opened and we turned as a nurse came in. She carried a clipboard and a jug of water.

'Morning,' she said. She looked at the machines and wrote on her clipboard, then she took a jug away and left the full one.

'What do you mean?' I said.

'Down there with Leonard. It was amazing.'

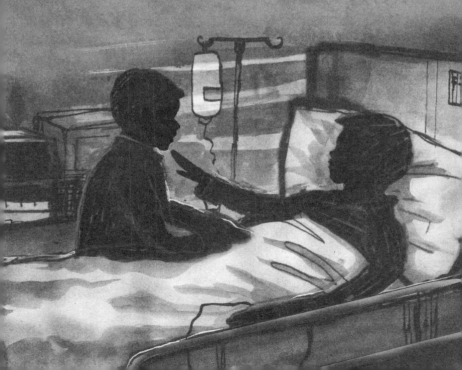

'Ned, did you . . . ?'

The door opened and Dad returned. 'There's my boy,' he said. 'How are we feeling?' He took Ned's hand.

'I've been better,' Ned said.

When Mum came back, her hair slick and her dirty clothes bundled under one arm, she grabbed me in a hug. 'Well done, Jamie.' Her voice was tiny and just disappeared as she went on. 'I'm so glad you're both . . . both . . . here.'

I didn't get to ask Ned any more about 'down there'. Grandad came to get me before lunch. Mum squeezed me in a hug.

'Can you bring me the Walkman,' Ned said.

I frowned at my brother.

'With that tape we were listening to.'

Understanding

It was a strange rhythm over the day that followed. Familiar things felt anything but.

I spent the afternoon with Grandad. Dad came to get me for dinner. I sat in the quiet, in the dark of the garage, watching the still water.

Sometime in the evening, I fetched my bike. It had been moved off the path and rested on a prickly bush. The front fork was bent, the paint cracked, the metal showing through. When I tried to ride it, I found the wheel had pushed back against the frame. Dad called it a 'write-off'.

In the morning, we returned to the hospital with clothes for Mum and things from home for

Ned. I took the Walkman and a determination to get the truth from my brother.

Mum worried about the food – Ned wasn't eating enough and there wasn't enough fresh fruit. She worried that he wasn't comfortable – 'Fetch his duvet from home, Charlie.' She complained that someone had opened Ned's window in the night – 'He has pneumonia for goodness sake.' Mostly she cried.

As usual no one spoke to me about what was wrong. I caught snippets of whispered conversation.

'. . . lungs are not recovering as we would hope.'

'. . . not responding to the treatment . . .'

'. . . not looking positive . . .'

Half the morning was gone when Dad took Mum to *get a coffee and have a break* and my moment came to ask my brother what was happening. If this was the end, I wanted to know.

Ned had other things on his mind. 'He couldn't hear me,' he said as the door shut.

'What?'

'Leonard,' Ned said. 'He can't hear it. I'm too far from the sea.'

'You opened the window?'

Ned scrunched his face. 'Of course. But he can't hear it. He can't hear the song. I tried to sing it again. But he can't hear it.'

I didn't know what to say. I did not want to think about what he was doing, or why he did it.

'Jamie,' my brother said, his eyes tugging at mine, 'I thought it was time.'

'Time for what, Ned? I thought Leonard was here for you. I thought . . . I thought he'd fix . . .

fix everything. Make you better. But he didn't. He hasn't.'

Ned sighed. He looked deep in my eyes. 'Jamie,' he said. 'In the stories, in Grandad's stories, no one got better.'

I stared back with my jaw set, holding in the tears. 'Atargatis, her children,' I said. 'They looked after people.'

Ned nodded. 'They did. They do. But maybe that looking after isn't what we think, what we'd guess, what we'd want it to be. Leonard *was* here for me.'

Silence a moment, and fear crashed over me in a huge wave.

'In the stories, Jamie – Mathew Trewella, Perla, the Japanese captain – they didn't get better. The stories ended another way.'

I shook my head at Ned. I couldn't hear this.

I thought I wanted to know. But I did not want to believe this.

I simply said, 'No . . .' and threw Ned's Walkman down on the bed.

When they returned, with coffees for them and hot chocolates for us, they brought Grandad with them. He came in holding a battered cardboard box.

I did not feel like games. I don't suppose any of us did. But Ned said we should play.

'This is the day I win,' he said.

Ned and Dad made one team, me and Mum another. Grandad went alone.

Grandad and Dad set the questions between them. Ned and Dad made a fearsome combo. Dad knew everything and Ned attacked like he had nothing to lose.

After they'd won, it was time to go.

Mum and Dad and Grandad whispered in the corner again.

'Jamie,' my brother said. 'Come here.'

I moved in a little closer.

'Here,' he said, putting his arms out.

I leaned towards him and put my arms around his tiny frame. He was smaller than ever, all bones. His little limbs wrapped around me.

'This might be it,' Ned whispered into my ear. 'I can *feel* it coming now.'

Tears filled my eyes and dropped onto Ned's thin hospital gown. I wanted to say something more, but all I managed was, 'Ned . . .'

'Thanks for being my big brother,' he said.

I squeezed out another 'Ned . . .'

'Come on, then,' Grandad called from the door.

Ned let me go with a grin and wink. 'This is the day I win,' he whispered.

Empty

Over the years, Ned had spent a long time in hospitals, under the eye of doctors. When he was gone overnight, I always felt his empty space above me.

Our room was colder. I was colder.

Every time before, though, I'd known he'd be coming home. I'd known he'd fill the house again. That night was different.

In the evening, the storm came. I imagined Ned watching the same lightning I did, watching it crack across the sky. He loved the way it stained your eyeballs, its imprint still there long after its death.

'Rough out there,' Dad said.

We hadn't talked much. He'd collected me from Grandad with a tight grin and red swollen eyes. We'd eaten our frankfurters in buns silently.

Like Ned, we both knew the storm was coming.

'What's gonna happen, Dad?' I said, not taking my eyes from the rain and stormy sea. I never asked. I was never told. But if there was ever a time for asking, this was it.

I heard Dad cough. I heard his silence. Then, 'It's . . . it's . . . it'll be all right.'

'OK, Dad,' I said.

I knew he was lying. I'm sure he knew I was too.

The TV went on behind me with a crackle and fizz. I recognised the voice of the host of *A Question of Sport*.

I didn't really like sport. Ned had always been the physical one, as much as he could be.

He watched *A Question of Sport* with Dad, while I read. If the Risk questions had been about sport, Ned would have always won.

David Coleman, the host, was asking Daley Thompson, '*Who won the silver medal in the fifteen hundred metres at the Moscow Olympics?*'

Daley couldn't remember '*for the life of him.*'

Dad was making a *hmm* noise.

'Was it Allan Wells?' I said.

'He's a sprinter,' Dad said. 'Fifteen hundred is middle distance. I think it was the German . . . er . . . Straub.'

'*The fifteen hundred metres silver medal was won by Jürgen Straub,*' David Coleman said.

'One–nil to me,' Dad said.

I turned to him with a grin.

'Come here,' he said.

199

I pulled myself away from the window and sat with Dad where Ned usually did. Dad put his arm around me.

By the end of the show, the score was eighteen–three. Dad said it was a good effort. He kissed me on the top of the head and said, 'Bed, I reckon.'

The bedroom was filled with Ned's absence. I replayed Ned's words again and again. '*They ended another way.*' My mind was filled with those stories of mermaids. I tried to see what Ned saw.

And still the storm raged outside.

Storm

The phone was ringing.

It just kept ringing.

The wind blew. The rain drummed. The phone rang.

I listened as Dad crunched down the stairs. There was a click. It rang out over the storm.

Dad coughed, then, 'Hello.' The word crackled with sleep. 'What?' There was alarm in his voice.

I stared straight up at the emptiness above where Ned was not. A tear spilled from my eye.

'What do you mean?'

I knew it was Mum on the end of the line and I thought I knew what she was saying. I thought

I knew what Ned felt was coming. I thought I knew until . . .

'Where's he gone? Why's he not in his bed?'

I pushed myself up and rubbed my eyes on the duvet.

'I'm coming,' Dad shouted, then the phone clunked down. I was out of my room when Dad called, 'Jamie!'

'Ned's gone?' I asked.

Dad coughed again as if to fill the silence Ned left. 'We've got to go.'

We stayed in our pyjamas, coats over the top, flapping cuffs tucked into socks.

'Where would he go, Jamie?' Dad said as he laced up his work boots.

A hundred places flashed through my mind. Hills and fields. Beaches and hidden coves.

Dad pulled the door open. A wind blew in.

The rain still drummed, fingers on the roof and windows. The sea roared. And through it all I heard a woven note, a song.

I knew then, without a doubt, where my brother was. I knew whose voices were carried on the wind. I understood then, Leonard and mermaids and everything. I knew what happened at the end of all those stories.

Ned was right. No one got better. Not Mathew. Not Perla. Not the Japanese captain.

I was right too. In the stories, when the mermaids came, they did take the sickness. But they took the people too. The waves swallowed them. The sea washed them away and left just a song, just a shadow, just an imprint in your eyes.

I ran. The rain swallowed me. The emptiness left and the song filled me.

The song filled me and lifted me. I swam

through the rain. I didn't bother with Ned's bike. I followed the song and Dad followed me, calling.

He didn't know the path like I did. He had not sped down it in the rain just a few days before.

Thunder rumbled.

Dad called, 'Jamie!'

I ran and Dad chased.

As I grew closer, the song grew louder. The rain's pitter-patter became its beat, and the roar of the sea melted into those notes. Those voices sung together. Thunder was their crashing cymbal.

I slipped and skidded down the path.

Dad called, 'Jamie.'

I called, 'Ned.'

Our voices clashed with the song. We had no part in that melody.

I did not miss the turn this time; it was marked by a discarded bike that I guessed Ned had stolen from some nurse or doctor working a night shift. I was off the path and on the rocks, calling behind me, 'This way, Dad.'

As I skipped across the wet slabs, the clouds broke. A splinter of moonlight shone down and its beams bounced off the water and reflected off two slick bodies, two tiny frames, crouched on the edge of the platform, where my world ended and the sea began.

Déjà vu. That's French for 'already seen' – a moment you've already experienced.

I shouted, 'No!' As I called, the thunder peeled and my voice was lost. That was the final crash. The cymbals rang out. The sea's roar died. The rain became a hiss. Tiny limbs stretched out. Together they dived. Ned and Leonard, Leonard and Ned hit the sea as one.

There was silence.

Swallowed

There was silence.

There was silence. Then a ringing. Then a shout – my name again and again. A low rumble began in my chest. It rose to pounding drums. The sea roared and I roared back.

'NO! NED!'

One step. Two steps. I threw myself off the edge of the world and into the black. I was swallowed whole by frozen jaws.

The water swum around me. I looked down on myself floundering, or I remembered looking down on the policeman in this same sea. I looked up at my face shining down – or was that a single star, lonely above?

A wave hit me and turned me. I held my breath and flailed one way, another. I called noiselessly into the deep, 'NED!'

I saw black and black, and as the sea turned me again and again, that lonesome star. No brother. No merman. They were gone.

The sea had swallowed them. Now it would swallow me.

Grandad nearly drowned once. At the end, he said, you felt something close to sleep. That floaty feeling where the world is lost and it's just you and a tingle in your toes and a whispered word running round and round your head.

I heard Ned then. 'Rabbit, rabbit, rabbit,' he whispered.

I smiled at the end. Icy water filled my mouth and I surrendered to the waves.

Then something grabbed me. A thick eel of an

arm wrapped around my chest. It pulled me. It dragged me. For the first time since I'd left the world, I resurfaced, choking and coughing.

Dad heaved us both up and out of the sea onto the rocks. My head fell back not against the hard rock but onto something soft.

'What the hell are you doing, Jamie?' My dad was crying.

I looked up at him. I didn't speak but reached back, beneath my head to the clothes bundled on a pair of scuffed plimsolls.

Dad scrabbled for them. 'Where's Ned? Where is he?' Dad scanned the sea, left and right and out towards the horizon. He wrenched at his boots.

Ned's words came to me – *This is the day I win.*

'Don't, Dad. He's gone,' I shouted. Then in a whisper, 'It was what he wanted. This is how he wanted it.'

I knew it was true. Ned had felt it coming as I'd fooled myself that it would be any other way. A child of Atargatis had come, the sea had called and Ned had answered.

Dad stood on the edge and stared. There was nothing to see but the waves, throwing themselves against the rock.

Dad put his hands up against his face and screamed, 'NED!' He went to dive, but I grabbed him and clung to him.

We looked at one another through the rain and the sea's spray and our tears. I knew my brother was gone as certain as the night, as certain as the storm.

Dad did not. He pushed me away with two words – 'Stay here' – then turned and dived into the freezing sea, into the dark. He was gone for a long minute while the rain poured and the heavens thundered.

When he appeared again, on the surface, ten metres from the rock, he called above the waves, 'Where, Jamie? Where did you see him go?'

I pointed to the spot and Dad dived again.

I did not move but for the shivers that shook my body. I stayed that way, peering out to sea, as Dad dived, again and again and again.

Each time he rose, he called to the deep, deep sea, 'Ned!'

Message

I don't know how many times Dad dived. I could have stood a year on that rock with Ned's empty clothes beside me and the loneliest star looking down from above.

Eventually Dad hauled himself from the waves. We did not speak as Dad gathered up Ned's wet bundle. He took my hand and we ran home, our pyjamas dripping with sea and rain.

The front door was still open, spilling out light. Dad threw Ned's things on the sofa.

I stripped and dried and fetched clean clothes while Dad phoned the coastguard.

Then he phoned the hospital. He talked to a nurse and another nurse before he got through to

Mum. Dad held onto his tears. He told Mum. And a wail sounded down the phone.

He told Mum the coastguard were out looking. He said we'd go to get her.

Every word sounded hollow.

He left me on the sofa and went to dry and change.

Beside me, Ned's clothes sat, filling the room with the salty scent of the sea. There amongst them was the glimpse of something shiny. Something plastic. I pushed his T-shirt and jeans aside. Wedged in his shoe was the Walkman. I pulled it out and shook it.

It was mostly dry.

I made sure the volume was low and clicked play.

There was a familiar hacking cough. I heard the thunder and the sea and rain. Then Ned spoke.

'*This is the end, Jamie. I know it's not what you wanted, not what you expected. If I could have stayed, I would have. But this was the only way to win, Jamie. I had to risk it all. I had to boldly go. These are your adventures now. Your continuing mission.*'

He didn't do his Captain Kirk voice. It was just Ned, alive as ever. I could see his lips twitching in a smile.

'*You've got to continue. Explore strange new places. Seek out new life and junk on the beach.*'

He stopped then. The thunder sounded.

'*Most of all, Jamie, do the same—*' my brother said, with his last message for me. '*Boldly go.*'

Salty tears ran down my cheek and into my mouth. I picked up the Walkman to hurl it against the wall but found myself pulling it to my chest.

Ned told me then to press stop. He had

messages for Mum and Dad and Grandad – he said they were too soppy for my ears. I pressed stop as Dad returned.

Dad looked at my eyes, full of tears, then down at the Walkman in my hands.

'Ned?' he said.

I nodded.

Outside the storm still rumbled.

Doubt

The coastguard had not found anything after a day and a night of searching. I didn't expect them to.

Mum did. She wailed and screamed, and her face grew ever more red from her eyes outwards.

Dad had frozen. His jaw was locked. He didn't look at anything. Not the coastguard or Mum or me or Tony who stood with his helmet under one arm.

'He was seen entering the sea.' One of the coastguard glanced at me as he said this, eyebrows raised.

I nodded.

'We'd normally have found a body by now.' He paused here.

Mum's hands were clenched, her knuckles white.

'Of course, we will continue searching for . . . well, for as long as . . . as is necessary. But . . .'

The coastguard man looked at the policeman. Mr Taylor nodded.

'. . . there can be little doubt that your son is . . . is gone.'

Then screaming. Dad showed the coastguard out. Mr Taylor made tea which nobody drunk.

There can be little doubt. Little doubt.

'*Down there . . . it was amazing,*' Ned had said.

Down there. What had he seen? All I'd seen was the dark.

In the stories, those left behind, like me, were left in the dark. The Japanese captain had seen something down there, but not his crew. Long Ben had only heard a snatch of that other world, in the song of the ocean. The brother had watched as

Mathew Trewella went somewhere he could never follow. I was left in the dark as I had been from the day Leonard came. I was in the dark and Ned was gone, gone for sure. But had he *gone* gone? Or was he somewhere? Somewhere down there. Would he still sing, like Mathew, like Perla?

There was doubt. There were questions.

That night after the coastguard had come, Dad asked me if I'd known what Ned was planning. It was an important question. I was honest. I hadn't known. But maybe I should have known. Maybe if I had not been so blind, if I'd believed what I would not. Maybe I could have stopped him.

Mum held onto me tightly as she wept.

'I don't understand,' she sobbed into the top of my head.

I wanted to tear away from her. I wanted to

scream. I wanted to smash each and every one of the *Star Trek* videos that stared at me from their shelf.

Grandad looked grim. He cleared his throat and said that nobody was ready to lose Ned. 'But he was always his own little man. Headstrong. He knew he was going. He made a choice to go his own way.'

I couldn't tell them about Leonard. I wished I could. I wished I could give Mum answers. But no one would understand. Grandad would blame himself for his stories. Dad would think I'd gone mad with grief.

I couldn't say, 'He might still be out there somewhere.' I could not tell them to listen, listen every night for his voice carried on the wind, on the waves. I could not tell them to listen for him as I was doing.

*

Over the days that followed – empty days, hollow, silent days – it wasn't grief that drove me, it was anger. I was furious with Ned. But most of all I burned with hatred for Leonard.

I took my brother's bike down that path again. I left it and hopped from rock to rock out to the shelf. I leaned out over the sea. I stared and stared into the waves.

'Why didn't you tell me?' I shouted. 'Why didn't you tell me what he was here for? What you planned?'

I shook, not with the cold but with rage.

'You said it was our adventure. It was not ours. You went alone! You went *alone*, NED!'

I roared my brother's name and the sea swallowed it as it had swallowed him.

I whispered now, but I knew the waves were

listening, for the sea had stilled and the world froze to listen. 'I need to know if you got there, down there. I need to know if you got that different life.'

My tears made tiny ripples on the swirling waters. Rain followed them. I let it fall around me and over me. I rolled off the shelf and into the cold sea. I bobbed a while then kicked off my plimsolls. I let them sink beneath me.

Then I dived.

'*Down there . . . it was amazing,*' Ned had said.

So I dived. Deeper and deeper. But for me there was nothing down there. Just the dark and the cold. They filled me.

When I could take no more, when my teeth chattered and my eyes would not stay open in the stinging salt, I wrenched myself out and onto the shelf. I lay again, shivering.

The rain fell. It grew dark. The moon came, and with it that star. It hung above, alone. I lay below, alone.

A voice came calling. 'Jamie?' He moved slowly from rock to rock. 'Jamie?' he said again. Grandad pulled his coat off and wrapped it around me. 'Oh, Jamie,' he said. 'Come on.'

He did not take me home but to his house. He dried me and wrapped me in blankets. He called Mum and Dad.

'He's fine,' Grandad told them. 'I'll bring him on home in a little while.' The phone clicked off, then Grandad sat beside me. 'Can I say something about all of this?' he said.

Grandad never asked to talk. He just talked. I nodded, knowing he must have something important to say.

'When your grandmother died,' he said, 'I

thought I had two choices. I thought I could either cling to her, hold onto every memory, let them tear me all up. Or I thought I could let her go. Pretend none of it had ever happened. Pretend I'd never had a wife. Harden myself to it. Tear my own heart out. You understand?'

I nodded. I knew what choices my parents were making; Mum was being torn apart, clinging to her lost son, while Dad was as hard as the stone he quarried.

'It took me a long time to find another way. And I won't lie, Jamie, it was much harder than the other two.'

I looked up at my Grandad, who normally had a story, a tale to tell, but today just these few words.

'It's just called living,' he said. 'And you have to get on and do it. Otherwise everyone loses – two people, not one – and the life you had with him stands for nothing. You know what Ned would want you to do, don't you?'

I nodded again, slowly this time. I knew exactly what my brother wanted. I had my doubts I could do it.

'*Boldly go,*' he had said.

But I needed a final word. I needed a whisper. I needed to hear his song, if I was to do as Grandad said, to do as Ned said.

Goodbye

I stood and looked around at all the faces.

So many had gathered in the tiny church for the body-less funeral. Mr Taylor was there and Lucy and little Pete and their mum, Claire. Mrs Clarke stood in a black cardigan and black hat. Tibs was there. His dad had closed the post office for the day and was there too with Tibs' mum. Nearly every family from school had come. The kids all looked strange, dressed up smart. The teachers were there. There were some nurses and doctors. Quarrymen. Bill the postman.

Before the service began, Tibs came to talk to me. He said what you're meant to say. 'I'm sorry, mate.'

I shrugged and glared. I'd been forced into a tight shirt and too-big suit. Grandad had his hand on my shoulder.

'Do you think you'll be coming back to school?' Tibs asked.

I shrugged again. Grandad squeezed my shoulder. It's called living, I thought to myself. I nodded. 'I guess so,' I said.

'Good, mate. I've missed you.'

Lucy had joined us. 'Yeah, you should; we're doing this project about space at the moment. You'd like it,' she said.

Then the vicar walked behind the stand thing and the service began with songs and religious words. I let it wash over me in waves. Waves of anger. Waves of tears.

Mum cried. Dad sat grimly and greyly. Grandad went to the front to speak. I tried to listen.

'Full of life,' I heard and, 'unforgettable,' and, 'the gap he'll leave.'

After the service, everyone came to the house. People had made food and brought out drink. A line of people held onto Mum, who flashed a brief smile at me from across the room. Dad's icy frame cracked a little, standing huddled with Tony, a few tears dropping.

I slipped out of the back door and stood in the quiet of the garage. Leonard's tub was still filled. I thought about tearing all the stuff down, the shoes and cutlery and pieces of driftwood. I thought we could have a bonfire. I thought I could fill dozens of bin bags. I found, in mourning, I was more like Dad – I wanted to shut down. I wanted to pretend none of it had ever happened.

Ned was in every piece of junk, every piece of

treasure. My brother whispered and laughed and shouted in that tiny space. Memories clawed at me. I breathed in deep.

'It's called living,' I whispered to myself, went back into the house and brought Lucy and Tibs to see the treasure trove.

Later, in my room, on the top bunk, Ned's bunk, I fell asleep in moments.

Some nights, sleep seems to last for ever. Others, when you wake, it's as if no time has passed between when you closed your eyes and opened them again. That sleep passed in a blink.

My eyes opened and I sat up. A dream had woken me, a dream of Ned, in red *Star Trek* uniform with fins running along his head, webbed hands and webbed feet. He stood on that slab of stone where I'd last seen him. He whispered to me, 'Let's get the hell out of here.' He dived, like I'd seen him dive on the night he left.

So I took Ned's bike and went once more down to the rock shelf. It was not a race this time. There was no storm, but the wind blew and on it came a whistle. A hint of a whisper. I followed that whisper and with every pedal was caught up in it, was swallowed by it.

I hopped from rock to rock out to the final one, to the end of the world. I knew what I'd find before I got there. Somehow I knew. It sat on the very edge, as if placed by a hand reaching up from the sea.

I picked up the small bone whale and brought it to my chest. The wind blew then, stronger, the waves gathered and in their beating rhythm came a song. Not a whisper now. A song from far away, from the depths, a song that filled me, a song,

joy-filled and free. And that song was sung by a
voice I knew. It was an answer.

    Those knotted doubts unfurled. I looked up
and out, away across the sea. There was
life out there.

        Away south, one
star still shone,

Fomalhaut, the mouth of the fish. Lonely it was. And, in its loneliness, brave, bright, bold.

I breathed deep. I smiled once more. Somehow life would continue. I knew now, as certain as the sea's song.

'Boldly go,' I whispered, holding the whale tightly, and I turned back towards home, towards life.

Acknowledgements

Thank you first to God, for giving me all I have and loving me in all I do.

Thank you, my friends and family, Jonny and Gemma, for your constant support, advice and vast capacity to listen to me moan when writing's just not working. Thank you, Maggie, for listening to every idea I have and believing in each one and thank you, Laurie, for your example of how to be courageous.

Thank you, Penny, for your unflagging support and belief in my writing.

Thank you, Charlie and Chloe, for helping me find my mojo again, for your insight and your advice in making this book happen. Thank you everyone at Andersen for turning words into beautiful books and getting those books into readers' hands.

Thank you, Kate, for again taking my words and creating beautiful images. Your art is incredible and it is a privilege to have it between the covers of this book.

Thank you, Caleb and Rocco, my constant source of joy and inspiration. You make me laugh every day.

Finally, thank you to Chloe. Thank you for being my best friend. Thank you for putting up with the highs and lows of making books.

My Brother's Shadow

TOM AVERY

Illustrated by Kate Grove
Nominated for the Carnegie Medal

My name is Kaia.
I'm frozen because of what happened.
I'm trapped because of what I saw.

Kaia is frozen with grief when her brother dies. Life at
home is difficult as her mother struggles to cope, too.
But then an unexpected friend appears
at school. He's different to all the
others. Can Kaia ever find it within
herself to grow again?

'Full of tenderness and hope'
Lovereading

9781849397827 £6.99